Miracles in the Making

Miracles aren't just for the patients…

A job exchange between two of the most innovative neonatal clinics in the world throws brother-and-sister dream team Dr. Kirri and Dr. Lucas West completely out of their comfort zones.

As Kirri heads to Atlanta and Lucas welcomes a new colleague in Sydney, they're going to be miles apart but helping to bring joy and longed-for families to so many more with their new working partnerships.

Only, while they are used to making baby miracles with the help of cutting-edge science, the miracles *they're* about to receive have little to do with science…and everything to do with love!

Discover Kirri's story in
Risking Her Heart on the Single Dad

And find Lucas's story in
The Neonatal Doc's Baby Surprise

Both available now!

Dear Reader,

Thank you so much for choosing this book—a duet with the fabulous Susan Carlisle, no less! There are *so many* books out there to choose from, and I genuinely am a happy bunny to see you here.

Choices, eh? That's what this book is about: trying to pick the very best path for ourselves as we navigate our way through life. Sometimes, fate gives us a helping hand and drops people and situations right in front of us, hoping we take the hint. This is exactly what happens to Ty and Kirri when a research exchange trip turns personal.

I know I say this a lot, but I truly enjoyed writing Kirri and Ty's story. Who can resist a proper Southern gent and a feisty Australian heroine? Hopefully you can't!

I genuinely love hearing from readers, so do get in touch. I can be reached on my Facebook page and on Twitter, so reach out and say hello!

xx *Annie O'*

RISKING HER HEART
ON THE SINGLE DAD

ANNIE O'NEIL

HARLEQUIN
MEDICAL
ROMANCE

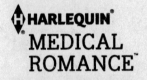

HARLEQUIN®
MEDICAL
ROMANCE™

Recycling programs
for this product may
not exist in your area.

ISBN-13: 978-1-335-14935-0

Risking Her Heart on the Single Dad

Annie O'Neil spent most of her childhood with her leg draped over the family rocking chair and a book in her hand. Novels, baking and writing too much teenage angst poetry ate up most of her youth. Now Annie splits her time between corralling her husband into helping her with their cows, baking, reading, barrel racing (not really!) and spending some very happy hours at her computer, writing.

Books by Annie O'Neil

Harlequin Medical Romance

Pups that Make Miracles
Making Christmas Special Again

Single Dad Docs
Tempted by Her Single Dad Boss

Hope Children's Hospital
The Army Doc's Christmas Angel

Hot Greek Doc
One Night with Dr. Nikolaides

Her Knight Under the Mistletoe
Reunited with Her Parisian Surgeon
The Doctor's Marriage for a Month
A Return, a Reunion, a Wedding

Visit the Author Profile page
at Harlequin.com for more titles.

This book goes out to all of those amazing doctors who pour their hearts and souls into making true medical miracles occur.

CHAPTER ONE

KIRRI LOOKED UP at the soaring skyscraper and beamed. *Unbelievable.* Her new workplace for the next six weeks was epically fabulous.

The Medical Innovations Center, from the outside at least, was everything she'd been hoping for. A towering testament to pioneering medicine. Maybe the doctors here would see what her brother couldn't. Dreams *could* become reality if she worked hard enough.

So what if it was pouring down with rain and she looked like a drowned rat? She wasn't here to look hot. She was here to set her brain alight. She was in Atlanta, Georgia, baby!

Ah...spring. Wet and warm. Such a contrast to back home in Sydney, where people were deciding whether or not to turn the central heating on. If everything went according to plan her research would blossom in tandem with the Georgia peaches.

Mmm... She inhaled a big lungful of Georgia

air. Totally different from the salt-laced breezes back home. It was more…floral. Jasmine? Honeysuckle? Who knew? She had six weeks to find out. If she ever left the lab, that was. From the brainboxes alleged to be inside it, she was pretty sure she'd have to be dragged out when the research exchange was over.

She tipped her head back further, then opened her eyes wide against the rain. In this weather, and from this angle, it really did look as if her new office building's rooftop was tickling the heavens. All glass and steel, the ultramodern building that housed the Piedmont Women and Baby Pavilion screamed trailblazing, forward-thinking, state-of-the-art medicine. It was *her* kind of place. The pinch herself variety.

Still a bit jet-lagged from the long-haul flight, and too excited to sleep, she'd come in early. Sunrise early. And perhaps three entire days early on top of that. She wasn't technically meant to start until Monday—but who needed settling-in time when she was about to embark on a last-ditch attempt to prove to her brother she'd been right all along?

It would be hitting sunset o'clock back home, where her brother was no doubt pounding out furious email after furious email. Or silently fuming even as his genius continued to dazzle their illustrious patient list. So she hadn't strictly cleared the trip with him. Or hung around to see what his reaction to her absence would be.

She'd covered all her bases. Put replacement neonatal surgeons in place—all of them desperate to work with Australia's so-called Baby Whisperer. Being his kid sister was handy sometimes. But at other times—like most of the time—less so. Like right now, for instance.

If she'd thought her chances of getting him to change his mind about pulling the plug on her research had been slim a week ago they'd be non-existent now. Her lab—her broom closet, more like—would remain dark and untouched for the duration of her absence. The type of research she was doing was not the Harborside Fertility and Neonatal Center's jam. But it should be, because bringing healthy babies into the world was.

She resisted the urge to check her phone, wrung out her hair and swept away another stream of raindrops to gaze at the place that had offered her and her research a lifeline.

She squinted against the increasingly heavy rain as a helicopter with a bright red cross on its underbelly swept in from the mid-level cloudbase and began to descend to the rooftop. Her heart began to pump with that telltale adrenaline that came with any medical emergency.

She'd never admit it to her brother, but the crystal-clear focus that came with performing life-or-death surgery was something she'd find hard to put to the side for the next six weeks. Surgery in the day, research at night. That was her life and she'd always liked it that way.

Right up until Lucius had pulled the plug on her DIY lab.

The invitation to come here and devote herself to research had been all the nudge she'd needed. A chance to make her dreams come true? Hell, yeah!

The helicopter disappeared out of sight as it settled on the roof. Her eyes dipped a smidge to the floor, to her temporary home away from home. *Clever,* she thought. Putting the Piedmont Women and Baby Pavilion on the top floor of the pre-eminent medical facility. Easy access to the roof and the clinic's most critical patients. Everyone must have wanted *that* prime real estate.

Heart, lungs, ears, nose, throat… This building had specialists for everything and everyone. But not a single one of them apart from the Piedmont Women and Baby Pavilion offered fetal and neonatal surgery. Inside its doors she'd be able to tap the brains of some of the world's leading neonatologists. And she couldn't wait.

Her brother would have said that the rainy day was a sign of misery yet to come, but she knew better. Beyond the clouds the Georgia sky would be every bit as blue as Sydney's, and when night fell there would be an entirely new set of stars overhead. Hopefully they were aligned in her favor.

Just as she was about to head into the main reception area a man raced past and bashed into her shoulder.

"Easy there, mate. You won't miss the parade!"

She whirled to face him and in so doing lost her balance. The basher reached out to steady her, one hand holding her upright until he was sure she was all right, the other holding an umbrella aloft.

Oh, my.

He was rather good-looking. Especially if "rather" meant drop-dead gorgeous of the possibly Latin, possibly Clark Kent variety of gorgeous. This was sexy-nerdy on a whole new level.

"I do beg your pardon, ma'am. Are you all right?" Superman asked.

She mumbled something. She wasn't sure what. His fault, really. For being so…*mmm*…

"Ma'am? Is everything okay?"

Kirri opened her mouth but nothing came out. Why couldn't she talk? She was a thirty-seven-year-old highly qualified surgeon, for heaven's sake. She had the power of speech.

She tried again.

Nope. Nothing.

If she hadn't looked into his chocolatey brown eyes and gone all gooey inside she would have been *completely* capable of giving him a piece of her mind for not watching where he was going. It wasn't as if the plaza in front of the medical center was teeming with people.

She would have done that. Told him off. She definitely would. But he was just her type.

Thinking the words gave her a proper slap back into reality. She didn't *have* a type. Not now, anyway. And she was far too busy to date, but…

She would bet actual cold hard cash that Superman, here, had been one of the nerdy kids back in the day. The type who got perfect grades, never got in trouble, was rotten at sports and the opposite sex paid no attention to. A bit like her. The type of nerd who never got asked to dance. She would've danced with him. And gloried in his transformation as he became an adult.

Athletically built with neat ebony-black hair, a speckling of salt and pepper at the temples. Bone structure a model would die for, a cheeky little divot in the center of his chin and those *eyes*. Espresso-brown with hints of gold.

He'd lived. She could see that by the small fan of crinkles arrowing out from his eyes as he narrowed them. Either that or he was using his special X-ray vision to ensure she was all right. Or checking out her bra. Perriwinkle blue lace, if he was interested. Front clasp, if he needed more details.

He blinked. Something quite different from lust was illuminating those flecks of gold.

Recognition.

She didn't know how, or why, but it was as if he saw straight through to her heart. If she'd had properly functioning ovaries they'd be working double-time about now.

And then, in another blink of an eye, he was a stranger again.

He gave a swift apologetic wave, pointed upwards, as if the gesture would explain why he was so distracted, then turned to go.

Fair enough, mate. We've all got things to do. But...nice to meet you.

As if he'd heard her he doubled back, handed her his huge golf umbrella and then, in one of those caramel-rich accents she'd only ever heard on television, said, "My heartfelt apologies. May I offer this as consolation for my rudeness?"

And then he disappeared into the building.

Mercy.

Half of her was tempted to race into the building and get trapped in the lift with him for the rest of the day. But the other half—the half she was far more comfortable with—wanted...no, *needed* to get up to her new lab and get to work. Twenty-four-seven if they'd let her.

She looked at the handle of the umbrella that

he'd just been holding, then at the front doors of the building. Tempting. Definitely tempting…

Her phone buzzed in her leather backpack and against her better judgement she tugged it out and looked at the message.

Oh, crud-buckets.

Australia's very own Baby Whisperer was giving her a right telling off, if the full caps message was any indication of its contents.

CAN'T HEAR YOU!!!

She typed her message back, like the kid sister she was, and then, reminding herself that she was a highly respected neonatal surgeon, deleted it and chose the far more mature option of ignoring it altogether.

She gave her shoulders a wriggle to shift some of her confidence from her heart through to her spine. Her father had always told her that aiming high wasn't high enough. Well, if pushing the elevator button to get up to one of the world's most prestigious research and treatment centers was anything to go by, she'd finally done it.

The Piedmont Women and Baby Pavilion was the pinnacle of neonatal care in the Northern Hemisphere. On a par with her own employer, Sydney's Harborside Fertility and Neonatal Center. The biggest difference was that her big brother wouldn't be her boss here. Not for the next six weeks. Thanks to the mysteriously enigmatic Dr. Ty Sawyer.

Somehow this premier neonatal surgeon had heard about her research and through one of his colleagues had offered her a lifeline—a research exchange. She'd have six weeks at his clinic and one of his colleagues would have six weeks at theirs at some point a bit further down the road.

The offer had been like receiving a direct hit of oxygen. Forty-two days to launch herself at a lifetime of sibling rivalry and finally prove she'd been right all along. That or go home with her tail between her legs and never hear the end of it from Lucius.

No pressure, then.

At least Lucius was some fifteen thousand miles away. She knew her big brother meant well in steering her away from research and back to full-time surgical practice, but there was something deep within her that needed to be *right*. She could be a forerunner in neonatal intensive care. Artificial womb technology was the key. Even if it *did* sound like science fiction.

So! New country. New clinic. And a once-in-a-lifetime chance to prove to her brother that she wasn't peddling false dreams.

She knew in her gut that she had the scientific clarity to give struggling mothers-to-be genuine hope that one day they could carry a baby to term. Hope and science *could* be bedfellows. Sometimes it just took a few thousand miles' distance from the naysayers to prove it.

She took a step toward the entryway, doing her best to ignore the nerves as they kicked in. There was no time like the present—and the present was now.

"Everything okay, Dr. Sawyer?"

Ty glanced up from the running water at the scrub station and frowned. "Sure. Fine."

He bit off the usual ending, *Why do you ask*?

Amanda, one of his top specialist delivery nurses, didn't miss much, and today was no exception. He was still shaken. Even with a handful of minutes having passed between running into that extraordinary-looking woman outside the clinic and now.

Bright blue eyes that looked as though they were being backlit by Hollywood... Rich auburn rain-soaked hair reaching halfway down her back... Lips the color of a burnished rose... Hip leather jacket... A fluffy, tutu-like skirt in camouflage fabric... And, if he hadn't been mistaken, because he'd been desperately trying to keep his eyes on...well, her eyes, a T-shirt with kangaroos dressed as cheerleaders on it.

The pompoms had been in an awkward position. Awkward for someone trying to maintain eye contact, anyway.

None of which was either here or there—because the one thing he'd definitively noticed was that he'd been attracted to her. And not just in an *oh, she's pretty* sort of way. It had been the sort of attraction that had gripped his vitals and given them a proper shake. A meeting-a-soulmate sort of shake. In other words something he thought he'd never feel again. Not since…

Well, he hadn't thought he'd ever experience that particular sensation again.

Despite his diligent scrubbing, and trying to assume what he hoped was his everyday demeanor, he could feel Amanda's eyes staying on him for a moment longer. And then, when he didn't respond, she went for a change of tack.

"Want me to run you through the details again?"

"If you wouldn't mind."

Details. Surgery. Exactly what he needed to take his mind off those bright blue eyes that had synced with his as if meeting the gaze of a long-lost lover. Madness, considering he'd only had one lover, but…

He scrubbed the thought away. His wife had been his one and only true love. Whatever it was that had happened this morning was clearly a freak occurrence.

He glanced out at the empty OR. The critical care transport team would be rolling in with the patient any second now. He'd seen the helicopter coming in to land and was surprised they weren't in the operating room already. Perhaps something had happened on the helicopter that demanded they take things slowly.

Though he'd virtually memorized all the details of the case Amanda ran him through it again.

Mary Lingford was an expectant mother. She lived just under a hundred miles outside of Atlanta, hence the helicopter ride in. With rush hour traffic starting as early as four a.m., they weren't taking the risk of her being stuck in an ambulance. At forty-three years old she was a high-risk pregnancy. She was twenty-seven weeks pregnant with a baby boy. And the baby, her local hospital had discovered last night, during a routine scan, had a congenital heart defect.

Hypo-plastic left heart syndrome. The most common lethal condition in congenital heart disease. About one in five thousand babies had it. None survived without surgery.

There were still a good thirteen weeks of pregnancy remaining, so Mary's baby needed to stay inside her. But that heart needed fixing. The Piedmont Women and Baby Pavilion was the best place for both of those requirements to be fulfilled.

Ty turned around so the scrub nurse could help him gown up. "Have they done any pre-anesthesia? I want to make sure they've steered clear of teratogenic drugs. Accidentally inducing labor at this point would be a nightmare."

"I called in last night, and an hour ago before they prepared her for the flight. No pre-anesthesia. They're leaving everything up to our team."

Ty smiled. There was never an i left un-dotted or a t left uncrossed on Amanda's watch. Extragenerous in this case, seeing as he'd scheduled the operation for early morning and she most likely would only be observing. She was a specialty delivery nurse. A skill they were hoping they wouldn't need this morning. But it was protocol.

The safety of Ty's patients was paramount. He went where most surgeons refused to go. Directly to the womb.

Amanda nodded toward the operating room, where their patient was being wheeled in. "Looks like they're ready for you."

Good. Ty needed to put his blinkers back on. The blinkers that had seen him through the last few years of his life. Through work and caring for his daughter and his extended family. Those were the three components of his life. None of which included having adrenaline spikes when he laid eyes on a complete stranger.

The telephone rang as he entered the OR. Amanda took the call.

"All right if Dr. West scrubs in?"

Ty looked up in surprise. "She's here already?"

Amanda nodded. "Jet-lagged, apparently. Said she thought it would help her understand the clinic's ethos if she scrubbed into a surgery and saw things from the ground up. Would you like an extra pair of hands?"

He nodded. "Why not?"

How interesting. He knew Dr. West was a surgeon, but from the sounds of her research papers he'd thought she'd be more lab rat. Someone whose world revolved around cell slides, microchips and Petri dishes. But it appeared he'd been wrong.

Good. He'd made a good call. A surgeon who wanted to hit the ground running? He liked her already.

Amanda wrapped up the phone call. After saying hello to his patient, and assuring her that she was in the safest of hands, Ty turned his attention to the anesthetist. Giving the patient the wrong type of drug could induce labor, thereby doubling the risk of administering anesthesia.

"Back home in Oz we try to go as minimal on the anesthesia as possible. Too risky for baby *and* mom."

Everyone turned as a feminine Australian accent filled the operating theater.

Ty's chest constricted as his eyes clashed with the familiar pair of bright blue eyes. Umbrella girl. Right there in the scrub room. Reminding him once again—or his body, at least—that he was still a red-blooded male.

Yessir.

Still vital and responsive, even after five years of certainty that his chances of connecting with a woman on that sort of level had died with his wife.

The woman tore her eyes from his, then gave the rest of the team in the operating theater a quick wave. "G'day, all. Sorry... I know I shouldn't be sticking my nose in before I've been briefed properly, but I presume the goal here is to keep the baby precisely where it is?"

This was Dr. Kirrily West?

Ty couldn't believe it. She wasn't the woman he'd been expecting. Not that he'd seen a photo or anything, but...*seriously?* Umbrella woman? And what was she doing talking about anesthetic before the very stressed patient was even anesthetized?

He gave his patient's shoulder a gentle squeeze and said in a low voice, "We've got a new surgeon scrubbing in but only as an observer. Nothing to worry about."

Mary gave him a silent nod, concern evident in her crinkled brow.

Ty looked back to the scrub room, ready to give this new doctor a piece of his mind.

Kirrily West wasn't wearing her chic biker chick ensemble anymore. She was in a pair of Piedmont scrubs, and making the standard-cut cotton top and trousers look far more interesting to take off than they should.

Why the hell hadn't he looked at her photo before he'd okayed that plane ticket?

No need to be a surgeon to figure *that* one out. He was a busy man, and looks didn't factor when he was considering groundbreaking researchers who might make an invaluable contribution to pre-term fetal welfare.

He caught himself staring instead of chiding as she swept her hair up in one hand, twisted it with the other, then bundled the auburn coil under a blue surgical cap. It was a simple gesture that made it far too easy to imagine many things he shouldn't.

Silky hair... Soft bare skin... A whispered moan...

What an idiot. He should have done that video conference call with her rather than tasking his colleague Mark with the job.

So that what? He could have changed his mind? Decided that a woman with a heart-shaped face and brilliant sapphire eyes that made his heart do strange things wasn't worth his time, despite her obvious genius and passion for neonatal surgical advances?

Science didn't work like that.

He didn't work like that.

Even so... The woman now twirling around for the scrub nurse to do up her surgical gown wasn't at all who he'd been expecting. He'd presumed she'd be... Well, *older* for one thing. Her insight into fetal reconstructive surgery was on a par with much more senior surgeons. Her take on what might be achieved one day in the world of neonatal intensive care was potentially Nobel-prize-winning stuff. Literally life-changing for countless premature babies.

None of which explained why he'd expected an old, frumpy librarian type. Smart didn't equal unattractive, but...

Oh, this was a disaster.

Kirrily West pressed her freshly gowned elbow to the intercom button again. "Any thoughts on the anesthetic front?"

"Dr. Sawyer?" whispered Mary, reaching for his hand. "Is what she's saying true?"

Right. Though only a handful of seconds had passed, it was a handful too many. *His* operating theater. *His* operation. *His* method of treatment.

He looked at Kirrily West and said pointedly,

"As our patient Mary, here, is awake right now, perhaps it would be best if we talk her through just how safe her child will be rather than focus on what hasn't happened."

He didn't know how they did things Down Under, but they did things Southern-style here. It entailed TLC and a whole lot more professionalism and tact for starters.

He addressed his team—and, most importantly, the *patient*. "As ever, Mary, our number one priority is your baby's safety. I'm not saying this is a routine surgery. It isn't. It's specialized. But this is the best place for you to have it and everything has been taken into account. Particularly the anesthetic."

Mary's brow was knitted with worry lines. "But what was that other doctor talking about? Will the anesthetic hurt my baby? I don't want to do this if the surgery is going to induce labor!"

She tried to push herself up from the gurney.

Ty resisted shooting Kirrily West a look—an eyebrows raised look, straight up to his surgical cap, that would make it clear to her that this was *exactly* why precision verbal conduct was every bit as important as precision surgical conduct.

But actions spoke louder than words, so he gave Mary's hand a reassuring squeeze and a pat. They both knew this was very likely her last chance of having a child, and he sure as hell wasn't about to be the surgeon to let her down.

"Like I said, everything's been taken into account and the protocol is as safe as these things can be. We're going to administer tocolytics. They're drugs designed especially to prevent premature labor. And I've just been told the emergency transport team administered an H-2 antagonist last night, which will also help." He looked Kirrily West straight in the eye. "Thoughts, Doctor?"

CHAPTER TWO

KIRRI GULPED. THIS was *exactly* the sort of thing her brother would have ejected her from his operating theater for. Leaping before she looked.

She called it spontaneous innovation. He called it foolishness. Up until now she'd thought both of them were a little bit right.

How on earth had she not noticed that the patient was still awake?

Easy. She was running on adrenaline and showing off for the hot doctor. At least Dr. Ty Sawyer wasn't there—the surgeon who ran the Piedmont Women and Baby Pavilion. That would have been unrecoverable.

Even so, she had to wonder if she could have made a worse first impression…

Probably not.

That's what happened when she showed off like a teenaged girl, hoping her nerdiness would appeal to his nerdiness, and then maybe—if pigs began to fly—she and Captain Umbrella would live happily ever after…

Struth.

If she hadn't been fully scrubbed up she would have thunked herself on the forehead.

Sheepishly she pushed the intercom again with her elbow. "Still all right if I join you?"

"Observation only," came the crisp reply.

Fair enough.

She'd been too keen to please. Too eager to prove she was worth the investment. And she wasn't just talking about the business class flight over. She was talking about being given access to one of the world's premier research labs, an amazing park-side apartment in the center of Atlanta and six precious weeks away from her brother to give her project one final push before deciding whether or not to give up the ghost.

Fulfilling one dream to make up for the loss of another was the way she'd rolled for the past few years.

Her hands hovered above her flat belly, then dropped to her sides.

Right. Enough of all these feelings.

She dialed back her nerves and entered the operating room. Whoever this doctor was, he wasn't impressed with her. And very likely he had the ear of Ty Sawyer, her benefactor. She had one shot to prove him wrong. Otherwise her packed bags would stay that way.

She stood to the side while Dr. Chocolate Eyes

spoke with his patient for a while longer, assuring her that whilst nothing came with a one hundred percent guarantee he would do his best to offer her ninety-nine-point-nine percent. Next he spoke with the anesthetist, then the pair of them together. He was calm, encouraging, and a picture of capability. It took a lot to impress Kirri but she was impressed.

Soon enough he was ready to begin.

Hypo-plastic left heart syndrome was a critical congenital heart defect, and performing the surgery to the letter was the only option. If he didn't fix it now, once the baby was born the left side of his heart would be unable to pump essential oxygen-rich blood to the rest of the body.

"Where would you like me, Doctor…?"

Kirri scanned the small group. There were three women and three men there. All gowned up. Only one with eyes that made her heart skip a beat. She looked away from him and chose a chap with more gray hair than the others. Could he be Dr. Sawyer?

A nurse nodded at a spot directly across from Dr. Chocolate Eyes. "Dr. Sawyer likes his spare pair of hands here."

Wait. *What?* Dr. Chocolate Eyes was Dr. *Sawyer*?

Oh, this was bad. The turn-around-and-jump-right-back-on-the-plane sort of bad. Why weren't there any pictures of him on the website? Normally this type of surgeons—the so-good-they-were-famous type—had pictures of themselves all over their websites, their literature. How had she managed to pick a camera-shy guy?

She checked herself. A woman who jumped on a plane and went to the other side of the world at the first whiff of a chance to prove her brother wrong should probably research things a bit more thoroughly.

Not that she would've refused the trip even if she'd seen his photo. Plenty of too-good-to-be-true men walked through the doors of their clinic back in Oz. Usually with a gorgeous wife on his arm, seeking the opinion of the Baby Whisperer to get the beloved child she'd put on hold after opting to have her career instead.

Lucky them. Able to put it on hold rather than spend their entire life knowing it would never be an option.

Kirri squished the thoughts away. Worrying about who her brother could and couldn't wave his magic fertility wand over wasn't her remit today. Making a fresh start was.

So… Dr. Chocolate Eyes was her new boss.

Okay. Fine. Just because he made her tummy do all sorts of curious things that other deeply scrumptious men didn't, did not mean she couldn't get a grip and focus.

So she took in a deep breath, calmed herself, and watched as the magic of surgery began.

A few hours later she exhaled.

Watching Ty Sawyer at work was breathtaking. It was like having a special glimpse of one of the world's best artists at work. Skill and finesse all wrapped into one incredibly talented package. No wonder people flocked to his clinic.

With little more than a microscopic glance in her direction, he'd left with his patient and gone to the recovery room. Now he'd returned, wearing a pair of fresh scrubs. Dark green. A nice contrast against his skin. He definitely looked as if he had a splash of Latin in him. It would explain the shiny black hair and thick dark lashes…

Barely meeting her eyes, he gestured that she should follow him.

Okay. She guessed they weren't going to go through the ritual. *How do you do? Nice to meet you. Sorry about earlier.*

Well, he *had* given her an umbrella. Maybe if she gave it back the gesture would melt the frosty atmosphere keeping him two briskly timed paces ahead of her as they virtually race-walked down the corridor to a stairwell.

"How're mum and baby?" she asked his back, then jogged a bit to catch up with him.

"Not too different from when you saw them last. As you saw, the surgery went well. The prognosis looks good. Her son will no doubt have more surgeries ahead of him when he's older… but it's a life saved for now."

She let the words slide into place with the weight they deserved. Easy enough, considering everything he'd said had slipped down her spine like warm, buttery caramel. How was it that the Georgian accent wasn't the world's favorite? She was its newest number one fan. So long as it came out of a certain someone's mouth.

A rather nice mouth, now that she could see it properly because he wasn't wearing his surgical mask. It was full for a man's mouth. Sensual, even. And tipped into a demi-frown that she could just imagine parting with her tongue—

Er…*no*, she couldn't! She could imagine no such thing.

She forced her mind back to more neutral territory as they zipped down the stairwell and opened a door to another corridor. This floor was quieter than the surgical floor above, which had what she liked to think of as the quiet hum of healing. This floor was obviously for the researchers.

Her heart-rate accelerated as she jogged yet again to catch up with Ty Sawyer and an idea struck. "You wouldn't happen to have the fetal echocardiogram, would you? The one they made the diagnosis from?"

He slowed his pace enough so that Kirri didn't have to jog. "It's on the system. Any reason why?"

She shrugged. "I geek out on that kind of stuff."

She threw him a goofy look, then tossed caution to the wind. She'd already made a complete idiot out of herself in front of him, and would very likely be packed off back to Oz by the end of the day, so why not go the whole hog?

"I kind of have a collection."

"Of echocardiograms?"

"Yeah." She risked a bit of a brag. "The earliest HLHS I diagnosed was fifteen weeks."

He gave a low whistle. "Early."

She grinned. Couldn't help it. She was the first to do it as far as she knew. Before that it had been sixteen weeks.

"I know. I think I was lucky. That or I have bionic ears. Anyway, I've got prenatal ultrasounds for pretty much every day of gestation and for all sorts of conditions. I thought it'd be interesting to have a look. Or rather a listen."

"Fine. But first…"

Oh, here it comes. The ticking-off she deserved for stuffing her bloody foot in it back in surgery.

Ty stopped in front of a door, crossed his arms and went epically frowny. "In future, if you scrub in again—and that's conditional—it's important for you to recognize hierarchy. And that begins with me."

Kirri barely contained an eye-roll. Typical male surgeon. Showing the little girl how things were done in the big boys' world. Yeah, she'd messed up—but she did have a few strings to her own bow in the surgical department. Thank goodness she was going to be a lab rat for this six-week stretch. Hot or not, she couldn't deal with being patronized in surgery.

"Right!" Ty clapped his hands, as if relieved the telling off was over, and gave her a quick once-over. The type a general might give a soldier before allowing him out onto the battlefield. "Allow me to show you our lab, Dr. West."

"Crikey. Dr. West's too formal for me!" Kirri laughed, but knew there was a bit of an edge to her narrowed eyes.

Ty had known in an instant he hadn't needed to tell Kirrily West off. Something about the way her eyes had blazed when he'd made his ridiculous "hierarchy" speech told him she was the sort who'd be beating herself up about it for ages without him fanning the flames.

"Call me Kirri," she said pointedly. "Not as awful as Kirrily. I've always thought it sounds a bit like a rash, doesn't it?"

Hardly. More like the trill of a songbird, Ty

thought, wishing like hell he hadn't gone all speechy. It wasn't his style. Nothing he was doing around this woman was his style.

"Right!" He clapped his hands again. Too loudly. "Let's get you to work."

Ty mentally kicked himself as he led her into the lab. Maybe *he* was the one who could do with keeping his mouth shut.

Watching Kirri introduce herself to the team in the research lab was like watching a peach tree break through the floor and blossom right in front of his eyes. Life where he hadn't imagined it possible.

Not that Ty's team weren't amazing. They were. Their hard graft and scientific know-how were at the heart of many a so-called "medical miracle". They were just…well, *quiet*.

"G'day."

She held out her hand and beamed at one of the lab-coat-wearing researchers. Malachy. The older gent was unbelievably intelligent and incredibly shy.

She pumped his hand up and down. "Nice to meet you. I'm Kirri. It's short for Kirrily, but Kirrily sounds a bit girly, doesn't it?" She skimmed her hands along her scrubs, as if she were a tomboy rather than a stand-in for a nineteen-fifties pin-up. "Not exactly girly material, am I?"

She didn't wait for an answer. She just laughed

and moved on to the next person as Malachy nodded and gave a dazed smile, clearly as awestruck as Jose before him, who'd reacted in pretty much the same way. Open-jawed. A bit overwhelmed. Not at all under the impression she was a tomboy. Nathan was busily cleaning his specs. Fogged up, most likely.

All sorts of uninvited feelings were careening round Ty's chest as Kirri worked her way round the room, her blue eyes occasionally flicking back, a bit nervously, to meet his. Admiration. Excitement. Disappointment. That last one was just for him, though.

He didn't like it that the one person in the room she was nervous of was him. Sure, she'd made a bit of a hash of things back in the OR, but it wasn't anything that he hadn't been able to fix. There'd been no need for him to go all icy and withdrawn. It definitely wasn't in his nature to be so cool, and he already knew he'd be getting an earful from the surgical nurses about not making her feel more welcome.

Apart from when she was around him, she didn't seem to have a shy bone in her body. She asked people who they were, what projects they were working on, begged permission to read all their papers so that she could be on the same page as everyone else.

If hurricanes were something you could wish

for, and came in the form of a beautiful woman who could work a room like a successful ice salesman in Alaska, this was Hurricane Kirrily in action.

Little wonder he'd felt blindsided when she'd swept into his OR with all that vitality. She'd reminded him of how he'd once been. Bursting with enthusiasm. Keen to make not only a good impression but the *best* impression. Feeling the sting when he was put in his place.

She'd come here seeking what *he* had wanted when he and his co-founder had set up the Piedmont Women and Baby Pavilion: a place where imagining the impossible was encouraged.

He stuffed his hand through his short hair and gave the nape of his neck a rough scrub. He'd been wrong to be so curt. To tamp her very clear passion for medicine. It was either envy or attraction that had made him behave like an ass. Or both. Not an easy pill to swallow when there were six more weeks of it to come.

Ty glanced down the corridor toward the stairwell. He had a full roster of patients today, and as everyone was used to him sticking his nose to the grindstone and then haring off late afternoon to meet up with his number one girl, today would be no different.

Except it already was.

He'd handed his umbrella to a complete stranger

because he'd felt something he thought he'd never feel again. *Connection.* There'd been something in Kirri's eyes that had touched him. He couldn't put his finger on it, but whatever it was it had felt like hope.

He looked out the window, beyond the leafy presence of Piedmont Park, and pictured his little girl swinging from the climbing frame or whooshing down the slide in her school playground. Tallulah. His six-year-old. Fearless, a powerhouse. *She* had a nickname, too. Lulu. Not that having nicknames meant anything. It was hardly a sign.

"You'll know, sweetheart. It may take a while, but you'll know. And for heaven's sake do something about it when lightning strikes. Our sort of magic rarely comes along twice."

His wife's words hit him straight in the solar plexus. It was the first time in years he'd remembered her saying them at all. He'd played them over and over when she'd first passed away— mostly because the idea that he'd find someone else to love the way he'd loved her had seemed impossible—but, as time had gone on he'd come to believe that she'd been wrong.

He wouldn't find love again. Not like that.

Gemma had been the love of his life. Cancer had taken her just short of five years ago, and the only love he experienced now was the fierce, protective love between a father and a daughter. And the love of his family, of course.

His four sisters and his parents had all but moved in with him after Gemma had died. Gradually they'd left him and Lulu to it, but they were still in and out of each other's homes so often they might as well all live together.

Loving them was enough. More than enough. Had been for the past five years, anyway. He wasn't experiencing a hurricane. Or a sea-change. Just a spring shower with an unexpected twist. Handing a rain-drenched woman an umbrella was hardly the beginning of a journey down the aisle.

"What do you think, Dr. Sawyer?"

Ty looked back into the room and realized half of the researchers in the lab—and, more to the point, Kirri—were staring at him.

"I beg your pardon. What was the question?"

Kirri gave an embarrassed laugh. "See? Didn't I tell you I keep putting my foot in it with the poor man! And now here's me throwing a spotlight on it." She turned to him and explained. "I was telling everyone that I looked like a drowned rat when I met you and you were a real-life Prince Charming."

She bit down on her lip. Hard. As if she hadn't meant to describe the scenario in quite that way.

When he didn't say anything she pressed on. "C'mon. Help me out, here. I'm really digging a hole for myself. You know…?" she prompted gently, a hint of warmth pinking up her cheeks. "With the umbrella? It was the icing on the cake."

"What cake?" Now he was properly confused.

"Getting the offer to join your brain trust for the next six weeks!" She said it as if it were the most obvious answer in the world.

Again he said nothing.

"Right! My chatterbox tendencies clearly need to be curbed." She gave her hands a swift rub. "What do you say someone shows me some desk space so I can find some room for my womb?"

Ty took that as his cue to leave.

Kirri blinked at the empty spot that had been filled by Ty.

Um… Okay…

"Does he always do that?"

"What's that, honey?" asked Gloria, a wonderfully warm African American woman with a slow drawl.

"Disappear."

She had been hoping to apologize for being such a nincompoop in surgery before he left. And for the Prince Charming comment. At this rate she'd have a rather long list.

Gloria batted her hand at the empty doorframe. "Oh, don't you worry about him, honey. He's delighted to have you here—he's just shy."

"That's one way to put it," said one of the men in a white lab coat. Malachy, was it?

"He's not shy—he was just distracted."

Yet another piped up. "He probably got a page. The OR is booked all day today."

Then the conversation took off in all sorts of directions until the entire population of the lab— about eight of them—were staring at the empty doorway in consternated silence. A silence only Gloria seemed brave enough to break.

"Mind you... I've never seen him like *that*."

"Like what?" Kirri was enjoying this more than she should. But getting the low-down on her new boss was a whole jar full of awesome sauce from where *she* was standing.

"Tongue-tied," said Malachy.

Gloria nodded in agreement.

"He isn't exactly a Chatty Kathy at the best of times," piped up another woman, Leigh, as she wheeled her chair over to a row of test tubes. "But it's true. He's normally not so...*mute*." She shrugged, then tipped her head to a microscope. "Maybe he's got a lot on his mind. It's been a busy week. And next week's even crazier, if what Stella was saying is anything to go by."

"Who's Stella?" Kirri asked.

"Surgical nurse," they all answered.

"She was probably in there with you today," one of them tacked on.

Kirri was about to quiz them about the surgeries Ty would be doing when Gloria patted the
desk.

"Why don't you put your bag down here and
we can take you on a proper tour of the lab. We're
all real excited to hear more about your research.
And, of course, show you our baby."

Kirri grinned. "You mean the 3D printer?"

Gloria's smile shot from ear to ear. "We didn't
think you'd flown round the world just to look
into some Petri dish."

Kirri felt an instant camaraderie with the
group. Petri dishes had their place in the world of
research…but 3D printers? They offered a gate-
way into modern medicine few things could.

She unshouldered her backpack, looked round
the room and grinned. "I can't believe I'm actually here."

"Dr. Sawyer is a champion of innovative medicine," said Nathan. "So, like you said, he's a real
knight in shining armor. For this kind of stuff
anyway."

He abruptly turned to his lab table and started
scribbling down some notes.

Gloria shook her head and laughed. "Don't
worry. You'll get used to us all soon enough.
C'mon, honey. Why don't we go and get you a
cup of coffee or tea or something? And then you
can tell me all about this baby grow bag of yours."

Kirri threw back her head and laughed. "That's a brilliant way to describe it. Much better than womb on a chip."

They walked and talked their way out of the lab to a small kitchen area, where some coffee was just being brewed.

"And this has nothing to do with artificial womb technology?" Gloria asked.

"No," Kirri said solidly. "I'm sure you know as well as I do that elements of AWT are mired in all sorts of ethical and moral dilemmas that'll take years, probably decades, to resolve. That's why sticking with the purely biochemical elements of helping premature babies survive seems to be the fastest route to making an impact."

Gloria gave her a sidelong look. "But you're not expecting any sort of major breakthrough over the next few weeks, are you, sugar?"

"Oh, no!" Kirri lied. "I'm just here to spread my wings."

And totally to have a breakthrough.

It was the only way she could garner some attention for her own rather primitive research lab and get some funding back in Oz.

"Good call," Gloria said, pulling mugs down from the cupboard and pouring them both a cup of steaming coffee. "Dr. Sawyer is real support- ive of that sort of approach. His specialty is, of course, surgery. But he's a firm believer in investing in innovation."

"Any particular reason why?"

Gloria looked at her as if she was crazy. "He's Dr. Cutting Edge! He got that way by going out on his own. Taking huge risks not many doctors would take. He wants to help folk who can see a reality that other people can't. There's a line a mile long to work in this lab. You're a lucky woman being eagle-eyed by Ty."

Interesting... So Ty was a surgical maverick? Having watched him today, it was clear he was highly trained in classical surgical styles. So much so it made her itch to learn from him. See the fetal surgical world through his eyes.

Gloria handed her a mug. "So. Give me the elevator pitch for this grow bag of yours."

"Well, first of all, I'm stealing that description." Kirri grinned. "Let's see... If it was a longish elevator ride, I suppose it'd go something like this: imagine a 3D printed womblike environment, hosted by a microfluidic cell culture chip that would ultimately serve as a replacement for an incubator."

"Good..." Gloria nodded. "And how would you explain that to the layman?"

Kirri took a sip of hot coffee, thought for a moment, then said, "The baby grow bag will revolutionize survival rates in premature births and help expectant mothers' health."

Gloria gave her a satisfied nod. "I look forward to being a part of that." She lifted her coffee mug to Kirri's and toasted her. "Welcome aboard, Kirri. May your research be fruitful. And don't you pay no mind to Dr. Sawyer. His head is always off and away somewhere. Unless he's in surgery, of course. And then he's your man."

She gave Kirri a little wink, then set off back down the corridor as if she knew a secret she wasn't yet ready to tell.

Her man.

The phrase knocked around her chest along with a strangely weighted sense of longing.

She'd had a man about six years ago. One she'd thought she'd spend the rest of her life with… right up until he'd dropped her like a hot potato.

He'd wanted children. She'd waited too long to tell him she would never be able to give him children of his own. When she finally had it had been as if he'd flicked a switch on his heart and turned glacially cold.

For the first and last time in her life she'd lowered herself to begging. Said she'd do anything to keep the relationship going. Adopt. Foster. IVF or a surrogate. But he'd lashed out and told her she'd *never* be fit to be a parent. Not with her compulsive need to be on a professional par with her brother.

He'd said it as if wanting to be the best was a *bad* thing! As if being on a par with Lucius was an impossible dream. It had been a cruel comment he had known would speak to the little girl in her who knew she'd never please her father.

She took a sip of scalding coffee and let the sensation burn away the all too familiar waves of emptiness as she headed back to the lab.

No point in worrying about it now. Her role in life was to help other women who *could* have babies. Women who could lead the life she'd always imagined having herself. And the only way she was going to do that and survive was by being at the top of her game.

CHAPTER THREE

THREE DAYS LATER and Kirri was finally opening her eyes at the right time in the morning. The scent of brewing coffee might have had something to do with that.

Coffee makers with a timer. Who knew?

Apart from utterly humiliating herself in front of Ty on day one, she was absolutely loving it here. There was a freedom in not being Lucius West's kid sister that felt positively liberating. Everywhere she went, she was just a girl in the crowd. A chick in a lab coat. No one to prove anything to—except for one deeply gorgeous, dark-eyed doctor.

She had *a lot* to prove to Dr. Ty Sawyer. The man had invested quite a chunk of money in her. In her brain, anyway. Not that he'd exactly been hovering over her in the lab, or anything. She'd barely seen him since Prince Charming-gate. Then again, it had been the weekend. Some people actually had lives.

Some people had someone to go home to.

She shook the thought away and re-centered herself. She wasn't here to flirt. She was here to work.

Speaking of which… She glanced at the bed-side clock. Time to get up and get on the road.

She rolled up and out of bed. The beautiful condo the clinic had provided her with was an amazing place to call home for the next few weeks. All glass and steel—a bit like the Medical Innovations Center—the corner apartment offered stunning views of central Atlanta and beyond.

If they wanted the place to act as an advertisement for the sprawling southern city it was working. Beautiful sunrises and sunsets… The lush surroundings of Piedmont Park in the heart of Atlanta…

Not that she'd seen much of the city center yet. She'd spent the weekend making good on her promise to read up on all the lab's projects. It was going to be a fascinating place to work. They were exploring every area of fetal development and beyond, and didn't seem shy of confronting wide-ranging and complicated issues like neonatal abstinence syndrome, fathers' stress in NICUs, oxygen physiology and just about everything else under the rainbow so long as it offered preterm neonates a better chance of survival.

She took a slug of hot coffee, stared out the window toward the clinic and gave a wistful sigh.

No doubt about it. She'd been hit by the "new crush" bucket. Ty Sawyer had certainly made an impact. Literally and figuratively.

What an absolute dill she'd been.

Room for my womb?

What had she been thinking?

Very little, obviously.

Weekend aside, she'd barely seen him since he'd fled the research lab.

Her more practical side told her it was time to shake off that particularly large chip on her shoulder. So what if he hadn't sat down with her to go through her research? It had been three measly days. Not checking up on her showed faith. Belief that she could get on with it on her own. Pragmatism.

Or abject horror that he'd hired her in the first place.

Even so… If the roles had been reversed she was pretty sure she would've invited him to a barbie, or on a guided tour of Sydney's finest offerings, or at the very least offered him a quick glass of beautiful Aussie wine to break the ice.

Maybe he doesn't want to break the ice. Did you think of that, Kirri?

The scenes of their brief encounters replayed on a loop.

There'd been a flash of something when their eyes had first met. Connection. A crackle of response when their fingers had brushed as he'd handed her the umbrella. The flare of it had blazed again when she'd seen him from the scrub room. Lightning bugs had danced round her belly and she was sure she'd sensed the same in him. But she'd thought the same of her ex. Thought the connection she'd felt zinging between them had meant they could weather any storm.

She put down the coffee and took a slug of ice-cold smoothie.

Delusion juice.

Her brother called it that when she'd appear, bleary-eyed, after another long night in the lab, wielding a green smoothie to be chased up by a double hit of espresso.

"Hitting the delusion juice early, are we?"

Lucius had had a point. He'd had lots of points, actually. Despite the turn of phrase, she'd always known he wasn't being snarky. He wanted her to focus on the job that she had. The one she was paid to do. Neonatal surgery. And she *did* focus on it. When she was doing it. The rest of the time it was all about holing up in the lab she'd crafted out of one of the old store cupboards, trying to tag team all the huge research centers that were also trying to create baby grow bags.

Or, in her brother's words, letting her life pass her by.

Up until the moment she'd boarded the plane to Atlanta her day-to-day existence had pretty much been comprised of surgery to keep her brother happy, research to keep herself happy, and sleep because… Well, that part was obvious.

Eating had happened. The odd night out with colleagues had happened. Dates rarely happened. Which was another problem. Because she didn't just want a child of her own. She wanted the whole nine yards. The doting husband. The cute little house. Nothing fancy. Just room for a barbecue and maybe an apple tree with a bench seat swing. A treehouse for the kids…

She conked her head on the breakfast bar and groaned. Her brother was right. She was on a full dose of delusion juice and showing few signs of recovery.

Creating a properly functioning artificial womb wasn't just a pipe dream. It was a constant reminder of the one thing she didn't have. A womb of her own.

She could joke, and wear tough-girl clothes, and maybe sometimes have one too many tequila shots, but the facts remained the same. Mother Nature had skipped over her when she was doling out baby-making equipment and it scraped her heart raw.

Mayer-Rokitansky-Küster-Hauser syndrome was a rare condition. She'd been born with ovaries, eggs and female hormones, but no womb. No ability to get pregnant. And there was nothing she could do about it. She'd never have a child of her own. There were, of course, womb transplants now, at a handful of hospitals around the world, but at thirty-seven years old, and chronically single, she didn't see the point.

Besides, the break-up with her ex had been so scarring she'd unwittingly begun to fulfill his prophesy. He was right. Her work life had rendered her completely unfit to be a mother.

The only counterbalance was knowing she was trying to help women who weren't in her rather fetching knee-high boots. Women who could *get* pregnant but struggled to carry the pregnancy to term. Hence the need for a baby grow bag, to nurture extremely preterm fetuses.

If she could develop it, it would be the most advanced neonatal incubator in the world. Not to mention that it would take fetal survival to the next level. There were other advantages too. Surgery, for example. Much easier on mother and child because they wouldn't be compromising the mother's life. And, of course, access would be much easier.

But, as with so many of these things, there was a complicated web of medical ethics to navigate and research was still—*ha!*—at the incubating phase. She'd be old and gray and maybe dead before it ever actually happened, so perhaps her brother was right. It was time to give up the delusion juice and start hitting the truth serum. She was a gifted surgeon, and if she really wanted to help she should give more of that gift on a daily basis rather than devoting herself to a pipe dream.

As if her brother had been reading her mind, her phone buzzed with a video call from him. It had been five days since she'd left. Maybe this time he was checking to make sure she was alive rather than detailing the terms of her contract in full capital letters. A contract she was very much breaking by being here in Atlanta.

But dreams were worth breaking a few rules for, right? So she pressed "accept", put on her cheekiest smile and grinned at her brother.

"Hey, Luci!" She always called him Luci when she wanted to make him grumpy.

"Hey, yourself, Maple Top."

Hmm… He was using the term of endearment he'd coined years back, because Kirrily meant leaf. He only ever did it very occasionally. He must want something. She braced herself for a speech.

"How's it going up there?"

Unusual… Chit-chat before laying into her. It was a tactic he'd never used before.

She played along. "Good. The facilities are amazing. Dr. Sawyer's got quite the set-up." She launched into a vivid description of the modern lab, the access she had to all the Piedmont research and how exciting it all was.

"More exciting than down here?"

Was that...? Wait a minute. Was her brother *missing* her?

"No, not at all..." she floundered. Because it was—a little bit. "It's just different. New. Nice to get a fresh perspective on things."

She could almost see the words arrowing straight to Sydney and crashing against her brother's solid stance. He still thought that the only thing she'd gain from coming to Atlanta were some frequent flyer miles.

"Right, well..." He scrubbed his hand through his hair and shook his head. "Thanks for sorting out the roster. See you in a few weeks."

Suddenly she missed her brother like she'd miss a limb. Sure, he was a pain, and they never had deep and heavies or hugged out their differences, but even if he wasn't a cuddly-bear-style big brother he always had her back. This call was proof that, no matter how cross he was with her, he still did.

"Thanks for ringing. I'll be sure and keep you up to date with everything here." Kirri swallowed back the sharp sting of tears, trying to keep her smile bright. He was a good man, her brother. She really needed to push herself hard at the clinic. Prove to him that what she'd done had been worth the risk.

"You take good care, then." He hung up the phone.

Kirri stared at her handset in disbelief. It was possibly one of the longest personal conversations they'd ever had. Usually just about everything they talked about at length involved the clinic.

Before she had a chance to think about it too much, her phone rang again. Kirri didn't even bother looking at the number and answered playfully, "Well, hello again, stranger."

"Kirri?"

Kirri's cheeks flushed hot pink. What was Ty Sawyer doing on the end of her phone?

"Dr. Sawyer! Apologies. I was just speaking with my brother. Sorry. What can I do you for? For you?"

Stop! Talking!

Ty, unsurprisingly, sounded confused. "We're a surgeon down today. Childcare issues. I was wondering if you might be up for a day in the OR rather than in the research lab?"

Was this an olive branch? Or desperation? Didn't matter. She was going to pounce on the invitation like a hungry cat.

"Absolutely. What sort of surgeries are on the roster?"

He rattled off a few in-utero procedures she'd done before. Nothing wild, but operating on a baby still inside its mother always made life interesting.

"Are you sure you're up for it?" Ty asked.

Hmm… Make microscopic advances in her research or spend all day making magical medicine with Dr. Chocolate Eyes?

"Of course. Definitely. Can't think of anything I'd rather do."

Especially if it got her in Ty's good books again. Even his normal books would be good. Whatever those were.

Ty Sawyer was still very much an enigma to her. And he might stay that way if she didn't start behaving like someone who *didn't* go all fluttery and googly-eyed whenever she was in his presence.

"Any particular time?"

"Whenever you can get here."

"Consider it done."

Kirri flew in and out of the shower, tugged on a lime-green A-line skirt and a T-shirt bedecked with a unicorn jumping over a rainbow and was out the door in a matter of minutes.

Once scrubbed up and in a surgical gown, she felt more grounded. The OR was her "can-do" zone. A place where she felt comfortable. Confident.

But hitting the right note was critical. A day showing the team what she was really made of would set her up perfectly for the next six weeks of research. And perhaps the next six weeks of Ty Sawyer.

Ty had to admit it. He was impressed. Three surgeries down and Kirri seemed indefatigable. She was a precision surgeon. Gifted, even. She approached repairing the most delicate components of a tiny infant's body as naturally as she might approach breathing. She was also excellent with anxious parents. Both the mothers who had to go into surgery and the parents who had to watch their infant children being wheeled down the hall on a gurney. He found those moments tough. Especially as a father himself.

Amanda had been right to push him into asking her to join them in the OR today. Just as well, considering he hadn't exactly given Kirri a warm welcome. Before he'd met her, he'd planned on inviting the visiting doctor to dinner with his family over the weekend. Taking her and Lulu on a cycle tour of the sprawling Piedmont Park. Pointing out the best places for that essential morning cup of coffee.

In short, he'd planned on pushing himself out

of his normal mode—recluse—in an effort to get to know the woman behind one of the most exciting medical innovations he'd seen.

And then he'd met her.

The lack of a specialized surgeon this morning had backed him into a corner. Get over himself or cancel the surgeries. He hated leaving patients hanging, so he'd relented and called Kirri, convinced she'd barely make it through one surgery, let alone three. But working with her was like working with an extra set of his own hands. Pure synchronicity.

They often had visiting specialists, and there was always some new little technique to pick up, or a different instrument to try. Sure, surgery was meant to be textbook—but someone had to write those textbooks and Kirri was definitely in that league. Beyond it really. She was the definition of "in a league of her own".

"So who's next?"

Kirri pushed through the OR doors with a fresh surgical gown billowing behind her, looking like a pop star about to dazzle thousands of fans. She was doing that, all right. Even if those fans were an OR full of nurses, anesthetists and surgical students. And, Ty had to admit, one single dad who had been figuring out the best way to tactically avoid her for the next six weeks.

Ty ran her through the case. A six-month-old

little girl, Meredith, who had gastro-esophageal reflux. The poor little thing wasn't getting all her nutrients and, more importantly, was in danger of breathing food or drink into her windpipe, which would irritate her lungs or cause infections.

They'd be performing a fundoplication. If things went as smoothly as they had in previous surgeries, the non-invasive procedure should have the little one right as rain in a matter of weeks.

It had been Amanda's idea to call Kirri when Ty's senior partner Mark Latham had called in, unable to come to work. His wife was out on the West Coast, doing some corporate lawyer thing, and one of his little girls was sick. When Amanda had suggested they call Kirri, rather than reschedule all the patients, Ty had balked.

Amanda had pressed. Said it was in the interest of their patients. They all knew that was the easiest way to get him to agree to anything.

It turned out Ty had had absolutely nothing to worry about. Kirri was every bit as knowledgeable, patient, willing to learn and talented at teaching her own deft surgical techniques as her reputation had suggested. She was so relaxed as she conducted the extremely delicate neonatal surgeries that she was even able to chit-chat.

She'd already won over the surgical nurses with her compliments about the facilities, their work ethic, their exactingness and, of course, their scrubs. They had fun scrubs here at the Piedmont Women and Baby Pavilion. Every color of the rainbow and each splashy print singular to the state of Georgia.

"And what do the green scrubs represent? That's the anterior retraction of the left lateral segment of the liver set. Could I get a Babcock clamp, please?" Kirri held out her hand for the device.

The nurse who handed it to her—Stella—answered for the team. "Oh, those are for the state amphibian."

Kirri's eyes flicked up to meet Ty's, and he saw a twinkle of amusement evident, even through her surgical glasses.

"The state amphibian?" she said dryly.

"The green tree frog," Stella explained, without a drop of humor. She took more pride in her home state than most. There wasn't a ball game with the letter G involved that she wasn't cheering for.

"Love it."

Kirri prepared the second incision. A three-millimeter cut that would disappear just a few weeks after surgery, if all went well.

"So, what are the other state emblems?" Quick eye-flick to Ty. "Suction, please. I'm just about to prepare the second five-millimeter port."

She did it swiftly and efficiently as Stella rattled through Georgia's other state emblems.

"The state bird is the Brown Thrasher. The fish is the Southern Appalachian Brook Trout." She listed a few more. The fruit—peach, obviously—the state flower, the state gem, the state insect… "And our state crop is the peanut, of course."

Kirri laughed. "The peanut?"

"Oh, yes," Stella assured her. "There's even a state monument. Isn't there, Dr. Sawyer?"

Ty threw Stella a look that he hoped communicated the following: *Would you please stop trying to draw me into this conversation? I know what you're doing.*

The nurses—Stella in particular—were on a mission to set him up with near enough every single female who walked through the clinic's doors. All those over twenty-five years old, anyway. Had been for the past year. It was as if they'd all decided that four years was long enough to mourn his wife's passing and it was time for him to pull up his socks and get on with the business of loving again.

As if it were that easy.

"Peanuts…" Kirri gave a happy little sigh. "I've definitely been through my fair share of those. Right, then! Here's the five-millimeter trocar—done. Are you ready to put in the neonatal gastroscope, Doctor?"

Ty nodded, his eyes once again connecting with Kirri's. There was something joyfully infectious about her energy. It was like that yellow brick road to Oz. Alluring, but frightening as well. The great unknown. Loving the same woman from the age of sixteen made the idea of falling for someone new little less than terrifying.

He had his routine. No need to veer from it now, when Hurricane Kirri was going to be back off to Australia in a handful of weeks.

"The next thing you'll be telling me is that there's a state-sanctioned barbecue," Kirri said, and laughed as she lowered her surgical goggles into place.

Everyone gasped. "But there *is*!"

Conversation erupted around the pair of them—Ty and Kirri—about whether dry rub was better or sauced barbecue. Beef or pork. And, of course, the more complicated question of what side orders to choose. Colorful language burst into play when someone said they were considering going vegetarian and were looking for the perfect way to grill an eggplant.

Kirri merrily worked away through the lively debate, with Ty serving as her second set of eyes and hands. And then someone mentioned Chuck's Charcoal Heaven.

Uh-oh. Ty knew where this was heading. He didn't hire the smartest nurses in the country for nothing, but sometimes… Sometimes they got the better of him.

"You go there every Tuesday, don't you, Dr. Sawyer? To Chuck's?"

Ty barely held back his *Oh, no, you don't*. Stella could sound as innocent as a child when she wanted to. Like a child asking if they were possibly *maybe* going to be passing an ice cream store when she knew damn straight that they were.

"They have some lovely barbecue at Chuck's," Stella pressed, clearly intent on making good her self-proclaimed role as his personal cupid. A role he truly wished she would relinquish. If he wanted to go on a date, he'd go on a date.

The unspoken lie gave him a sharp twist of discomfort.

"You'll know when you're ready, darlin'..."

He tipped his head toward Kirri and said. "Perhaps we should give Dr. West a bit more quiet space to conduct her surgery? I doubt the finer points of dry rub or sauce are of interest to her right now."

"Oh, no. Don't stop. It helps me relax."

One glance and it was easy to see she was smiling. Ty knew quite a few surgeons who liked music while they operated. He was a fan of country, himself, but it had been his wife's favorite as well, so for the past five years he'd operated in silence. Detailing Georgia's finest delights as if the entire surgical team were moonlighting for the tourist board was a new one for him.

Curiosity got the better of him. He had to ask. "Talking about barbecued meat *relaxes* you?"

"Not necessarily that topic, per se, but…" Her eyes flicked up to meet his. "This is going to sound ridiculous, but I like the sound of your voice. Your accent maybe. It's comforting."

Her gaze lingered on his eyes for a moment, then went straight back to the surgical screen as if she'd told him she preferred a harmonic scalpel over conventional knot-tying for the finer points of surgery.

Was it time? Time to let go of that protective shield of hurt and loss he'd wrapped himself in when Gemma died?

He heard himself ask, "Do you like barbecue?" *Nice work, Romeo.*

Stella threw him an encouraging glance and tacked on a *go ahead* nod. *Get on with it*, her eyes were saying. *We've got your back.*

"I love it—but you've got some tough competition."

"Where?" Stella gasped. "You better not say Texas."

"I think you'll find barbies are a national pastime in Australia," Kirri replied.

"You should take her to Chuck's, Dr. S," Stella said, oh, so casually, her eyes fastidiously glued on the screen, where Kirri was delicately wrapping the upper part of the baby's stomach around the base of her esophagus.

Oh, boy. And here it was. The awkward moment when he did or didn't ask Kirri out.

There'd be hell to pay in the debrief room if he didn't. And a strange new set of emotions to resist if he did.

He liked her. And not just professionally. But he had a little girl to think about. One who'd been asking about other little girls' mommies and what he thought it might be like having a mommy of her own.

He looked across at Kirri. Those blue eyes of hers met his as if she sensed he was trying to work out whether or not she was worthy of barbecue.

It was a much bigger choice than she'd ever know. Brave some barbecue or stay mired in a routine he knew needed changing one day. But… was *this* the day? Was this the woman he would change it for?

Kirri knew a plea for help when she saw one. Ty needed rescuing. She could see it in his eyes. Those shiny, espresso-rich eyes of his were virtually pleading with her to help him. The poor man was clearly being pushed into a set-up. It had happened to her enough times to know one when she saw one.

No matter how scrumptious she thought he was, first and foremost he was her lifeline to those all-important medical breakthroughs she needed to make. And as such she needed to tilt her lance. Or whatever it was knightesses in shining armor did when they were trying to do good. Turn and run away?

She cleared her throat pointedly. "Don't you worry about me. I can look after myself." She expertly tied off the final internal stitch. "All done. You can remove the camera now, Doctor."

His eyebrows lifted. "Finished?"

She tipped her head toward the screen, where one freshly sutured esophageal passage was on view. "Finished."

"That was fast." Ty began slowly to extract the camera as another member of the surgical team moved into Kirri's place to close up the small incisions.

"It was done to the letter," she said.

"I didn't say otherwise. I was merely commenting on how expedient you are."

"But not at the expense of the patient's welfare."

Ty's eyes hit hers with a flash of light. "I would expect nothing less. Not in my OR, anyway."

Kirri chewed her lip. It was the only way to bite back the snarky comment she would happily have flung at her brother if he'd said that.

Why are your hackles up? Because he doesn't want to date you? You don't want to date him. Or do you? Do you? OMG you do.

Quit having a conversation with yourself and let the man run his OR the way he wants. Get out of your surgical scrubs, get into the lab, make a medical breakthrough then go home and get on with things.

"Would you like to join me for some barbecue tonight?"

Kirri's eyes snapped back to his.

Say something, idiot!

"Um…"

Nice one.

"It's very casual. Beyond informal, in fact. And it wouldn't be just the two of us."

Everything that had been tingling around her nervous system dulled.

Ah. Of course he had a girlfriend. Maybe a wife? She hadn't seen a ring on his finger. Then again…he was a surgeon. Most of the male surgeons she knew didn't bother with rings, what with all the scrubbing up.

"My daughter and I go every Tuesday," Ty said into the yawning silence that was now consuming the operating room.

"Oh!" Kirri flinched at the high pitch of her voice, then managed to squeak, "You have a daughter?"

The knife plunged into her heart.

He had a daughter.

Ty Sawyer knew the precious love between parent and child that she would never know.

She knew it shouldn't hurt. Not anymore. It was as if the pain was built in now. A low-grade ache, reminding her of the relationship she'd lost because of a glitch in her genetics.

"Tallulah."

There was no missing the love in Ty's voice.

"Atlanta's biggest devotee to barbecue."

Ty stepped back from the operating table as the rest of the team silently moved in. Their attention was on the patient, obviously—but it was patently obvious that their ears were glued to the interchange between Ty and Kirri. So much so it felt as if they were bearing witness to a miracle. And it wasn't the miracle of modern-day medicine.

"If you're happy to leave from here, I tend to go straight from work. Six o'clock suit?"

She glanced up at the clock. It was almost three. Enough time to develop a case of the sniffles?

"Perfect."

It wasn't. She didn't want to go out with Ty and his daughter. She was always super-awkward with kids, too bright. She always ended up feeling like a freakish maiden auntie—which she'd also never be because her brother looked about as ready to have babies as her body was. Not at all. Which was weird, considering he adored them, but whatever...

Without so much as a tip about what one wore for "casual barbecue" Ty left the room.

Well, she thought as the rest of the surgical team threw each other a combination of winks and wide-eyed glances, *like it or not—it looks like I have a date.*

Ty tried to focus on the images on his computer screen and couldn't.

After the unbelievably awkward end-of-surgery "Would you like to join me for some barbecue?" incident, Kirri had fled to the research lab and Ty had holed up in his office with imaginary paperwork. Imaginary because he was finding it difficult to focus.

What on earth had he been thinking? Inviting her to eat barbecue with Lulu? A little girl who might easily think he was bringing along a candidate for stepmother. She'd never outright asked him if she'd ever have a new mommy, but he wasn't blind to the way she looked at the mothers at school events. Little girls were built of hopes and dreams. Hopes and dreams he hadn't let himself consider, let alone actualize.

He gave his scalp a short sharp scrub, willing some common sense to fall in. Maybe he could tech talk with her all night. That would put Lulu off the scent of what his body was telling him. He was attracted to Kirri. An attraction that was more than skin-deep.

A couple of hours later—strangely close to six o'clock—Stella tapped on his office door.

"Why, Dr. Sawyer, as I live and breathe. I couldn't find you anywhere. I thought you might've pulled a sickie."

He gave her a wry smile. She knew him well. He far preferred practicing medicine to sitting in his office doing paperwork. It was definitely the last place on anyone's list to look for him. Even so—a *sickie*?

"You know as well as I do that my mother would consider that awfully bad manners. I suppose your mama would too, Stella."

"That she would." Stella leant against the doorframe and smiled. She clearly wasn't through with him yet. "Well, aren't you just full of surprises? Asking our good Dr. West out to join you tonight."

Ty laughed and threw a sideways *get you* look at his cheekiest employee. Not only did she merrily cross the employee-friend line every chance she got, she was also a damn fine pediatric nurse. Being ribbed every now and again was worth each precious minute she treated his high-needs pediatric patients.

The way he saw it, for every life saved they put a bit more light back in the world. Light he needed as much as the next person. Because the day his wife had died near enough all the light had gone with her. And without his little girl... Well, that wasn't a world worth thinking about.

Stella smiled at him, fluffed her afro, then relaxed into an attitude he knew all too well: An *I told you I was right all along* face, quickly followed by a gloating smile.

He tapped his pen on his desk. "Isn't it funny how you just happened to mention barbecue and my nights out? All on a Tuesday, no less."

"Oh, it wasn't me who brought up barbecue. It was Kirri."

"Oh." He gave the back of his neck a rub. *Had it been?* "That's strange."

"Very," said Stella, a contented smile playing on her lips as she handed him a form to sign. "Some might take it as a sign."

Yeah, right. He handed the paper back and she gave him a new one. She had a stack of them and was taking her time.

"I just helped put two and two together, is all."

"If that's what you want to call it, Stella."

"It is." She smiled and made another exchange of papers. "What're you going to wear?"

He looked down at his cotton plaid shirt and khakis. "Dad gear", as his sisters relentlessly mocked. He bought it all online. Easier than actually going shopping.

"Been a while since you dusted off your glad rags, isn't it?"

"For barbecue?" He huffed out a laugh. "I'll wear what I'm wearing, Stella. No need to go black tie."

"Suit yourself."

Stella started humming. This was one of her favorite pastimes. Putting a mirror up to Ty's non-existent social life. She was always "casually" pointing out some lovely single woman she happened to know who was joining a group for tailgating at a ball game, or picnicking in the park—doing anything apart from work, to be honest. She said she wasn't pushing—just putting the invitation out there in case something better didn't come along.

Something better always did. Being with his daughter. She trumped everything. Especially his non-existent dating life.

Stella gave him a once-over and started clicking her tongue.

"What? I don't look that bad, do I?" He looked down at his clothes. Plain old khakis and a dull-colored dad shirt that probably could've done with a run-in with the iron.

Oh, Lord. He cared.

"Oh, wipe that look off your face, Ty. You look

fine. I'm just surprised it took you this long to show Kirri some proper hospitality. What with you being a proper Southern gent, and all."

Stella's smile was pure innocence, but he knew what she was saying. *You were being rude because you find her pretty.*

"I was planning on doing it. I just thought if I was going to show her Atlanta properly she might like something a bit more…" He sought the right word. *Was* there a word?

"Fancy? Classy?" Stella filled in, then instantly dismissed them. "No, sir. Kirri strikes me as a woman who'd be happy wherever, whenever. You just put Lulu in charge, pop a bib on her and have at it. She'll love it. She'll love *you*."

Oh, God. He hoped not.

He glanced across at his computer's screensaver. It was a photo of him pushing Lulu on a baby swing. She was young. Six months old. Laughing and smiling…at her mother.

It was the last time Gemma had felt well enough to join them at the playground.

He swallowed down the bile. Cancer was so cruel. So was widowhood. Five years and counting and he simply hadn't found the knack for it. Didn't know if he ever would. His daughter's sheer joy in life demanded that he live in the present, but there was a huge part of his heart still lodged on that awful day in the oncologist's office.

"Stage Four cervical cancer. Fairly advanced. It's up to you, of course, but we would advise delaying treatment until the baby is delivered, if you'd like to carry the pregnancy to term. But bear in mind doing so could affect your chances of survival."

They'd only just found out she was pregnant. Gemma had never had a chance of long-term survival. She'd chosen their daughter's life over her own.

She'd pushed through her pregnancy, and then nearly one more year—but that had been sheer force of will and probably a bit of blind luck. She'd wanted to see her baby and she had done so.

Saying goodbye after she'd fought so hard to bring life into the world—the life *they'd* created—had been the most painful thing Ty had ever experienced. He wasn't even sure he'd finished saying goodbye, if he were being truly honest. It seemed too final.

He knew some people plastered their homes and workplaces with photos of their deceased spouse. Talked about them all the time. Laughed when they recounted stories of the "good old days". He wasn't up to it. There were pictures in his daughter's room, of course, but none in his.

Or elsewhere. Hanging up Gemma's photo would feel like turning her into a shrine.

He knew she wasn't coming back, but he still hadn't figured out the best way to own his deep-seeded love for her and still get on with life. So, while he pushed everything else in his life forward, his personal life circled endlessly in the same listless holding pattern.

"Are you going to take her to the bowling alley as well?" Stella handed him another paper to sign.

"If she's up for it. As you well know, Lulu and I will be going regardless."

His Tuesday nights with Lulu were sacred. Well. Not that sacred. They often had people join them for the triumvirate of barbecue, biscuits and bowling. Family. Aunts, uncles—any number of the fleets of cousins that kept her from feeling like the only child she was. Plenty of folk from the office had come along one time or another too. Never once, though, had he brought a date.

She's isn't a date. She's a colleague.

He thought of the way his body reacted when he was around Kirri. Like one magnet to another.

Stella fanned herself with the rest of the papers and gave him an approving nod.

"What? Why are you looking at me that way?" he asked.

"I'm just proud of you, is all."

"Proud? For what?"

"Putting yourself out there."

He snorted. "I'm taking an employee for some barbecue and biscuits." He gave her back the signed papers. "And that's happening mostly because *you* backed me into a corner."

Stella shook her head, perched herself on the edge of his desk and leant in. "Uh-uh. I didn't back you nowhere. You *wanted* this."

"You'll know..."

Stella wasn't done yet. "Now, Ty, forgive me for butting in where I know you don't want people sticking their noses—but somebody's got to do it and I've given myself the job. I know your heart was broke real bad all those years ago..."

His jaw tightened. Yes, it had been. Smashed into a million tiny pieces, if anyone wanted to know.

Stella put her hand on her heart. "I didn't know your wife as well as you did, obviously, but I knew her well enough to assure you that the one thing your Gemma would've hated would be to see you alone for the rest of your life."

She tutted at him before he could interrupt.

"You are always encouraging people to change. Take risks. Push harder. Dig deeper. Travel...try something new! The only person I don't see doing that in his own life is you."

She held up a hand.

"I'm not talking about work. We all know

you're light years ahead of everyone else on that front. I'm talking about here." She tapped her heart. "I know you've got your daughter, and your family are amazing, but I've seen the way you look at her. At Kirri."

She stood up and put her hands out in a *Stop, I'm not done yet* position.

"She's here for six weeks. Have a trial run. That's all I'm saying. No one's asking you to fall in love or elope to the Caribbean, or anything. We just want you to have some fun."

Fun?

Wait a minute…

"We?"

Stella nodded. "All of us. We love you, whether you like it or not, and just like your family we want to see you happy. If a fling with a sexy brainiac from Down Under brings some light back into those eyes of yours I say go for it."

She left before he could say anything.

She needn't have bothered. He was completely and utterly dumbstruck. Have an affair? Just *because*? Merely thinking about holding another woman in his arms felt like betraying his wife's memory.

That familiar resolve set in. *Nope. Wasn't going to happen.* They'd have their barbecue, maybe bowl a few pins and that would be that. In fact he'd do better than that. He'd call in reinforcements. No way was this going to be a date, let alone the start of an affair.

From tomorrow morning it would be work only. End of story.

CHAPTER FOUR

Kirri felt like she was being frog-marched to her date. Ty was barreling along with that same crisp take-no-prisoners walk he'd used on their first day after she'd gaffed in the OR. She'd thought today's series of successful surgeries had put them in better stead, but apparently not. It appeared all this so-called Southern hospitality didn't extend as far as the parking lot.

"This is us."

Ty pointed at a comfortable-looking SUV in a rather daring shade of orange. Definitely not the color she would have picked for him.

He caught her funny look and explained. "My daughter picked the color. She said it reminded her of Pippi Longstocking's hair." He gave a *what can you do?* shrug.

It was a micro insight into a man who clearly liked to keep his private life just that. Private.

His eyes lingered for a moment on the car, as if he were seeing it anew, and the hint of a smile appeared. Against her better judgement, a little part of her melted. But she had a very strict rule: *Do not find adorable things fathers say about their daughters adorable.*

The idea of falling in love with a single dad— if he even *was* single—was… *Oof!* It would be inserting herself into a permanent reminder that she would never be enough. Then add on the fact she'd never live up to the ex—because no matter how awful she'd been, she'd produced a child. And, as her own ex's extremely quick marriage to a woman she would never have imagined him marrying, and subsequent rapid-fire arrival of three children proved, love *was* conditional.

So, no, thank you very much Mr. Hot-Maybe-Single-Maybe-Divorced-Dad. You carry on being all cantankerous and edgy. Suits me to a T.

They climbed into the car. Ty maneuvered it out of the parking spot, out of the subterranean carpark and out into the golden early-evening sun.

Her eyes drifted toward his hands on the steering wheel. Still no ring. No divot, even. So definitely not married. Dating or divorced it was, then!

Ty pulled the car onto the freeway with a comment about Chuck's Charcoal Heaven being twenty-odd minutes down the road before clicking on the radio. Excellent. Small talk was out. Less chance of her putting her foot in it.

It was a kids' channel. There was a song on about a penguin going for a swim with a dolphin. She couldn't help it. She cackled.

Ty shot her a look. Either he hadn't been listening or this was his playlist.

"Sorry. Didn't mean to offend. Is this one of your favorites?"

He frowned at the radio, then that soft smile hit again. "My daughter's."

Kirri laughed, then spoke without thinking. "Your daughter seems to wield a lot of power in your household. What else is she in charge of?"

Ty's grip on the wheel had tightened along with his jaw.

The look she received this time was barbed. It delivered a message she knew all too well. The *back off, you're not her parent* look.

She'd clearly overstepped. A blunt reminder of why she avoided lusting after men who had children.

Frustratingly, she felt the sting of tears tease at the back of her throat. Nothing like being put in her place by a kid she'd never met.

The over-familiar lash of self-flagellation whipped into play. *Why* had she made that stupid comment? It wasn't Ty's fault she couldn't have children. Parents were *meant* to be protective. It wasn't her place to comment on how he and his child did things. Not her place at all.

She forced herself into a more useful line of thinking. She should be asking all the usual questions. *What's her name? How old is she? Is her mom meeting us there or are you single and free for a bit of a snog later?*

She axed that last one with a bit of a smirk, but felt her heart sink all the same. Not only did she struggle speaking to parents about their offspring, she *really* struggled making chit-chat with their children. Babies were cool. Before two they couldn't really talk. And over eighteen they were much more difficult to imagine giving birth to. Everything in between: *#itscomplicated.*

Ty moved his hand to the radio to change the channel, then obviously had a change of heart and switched it off entirely.

After a moment's exceedingly awkward silence he gave her a quick glance. "Apologies. I barely notice the music. I tend to let Lulu pick the things she cares about, and I pick the things I care about, and as such my life doesn't often look the way it should for a thirty-nine-year-old man."

She snorted. "There's a look that goes with being thirty-nine? I wish someone had told me that earlier. I've only got two years to figure out what it is!"

His lips twitched into a smile. "Perhaps not,

but I suspect it wouldn't involve 'Itsy Bitsy Spider' on a loop. Or bright orange cars."

"Oh, I don't know..." Kirri felt herself warming to the subject. "I'm sure the powers that be would happily make an entire line of orange vehicles because of the fleets of children who adore Pippi Longstocking. As a sort of redhead, you can count me amongst the converted."

She was a Pippi aficionado, so could happily discuss her for hours should the need arise.

"Noted," said Ty, and nodded, that smile of his still playing on his lips.

Mercy, he was sexy when he wasn't frowning, and even then...

"You'll have to forgive me, Kirri. I shouldn't have been short with you. It's not the way I normally treat new colleagues when I take them out for barbecue."

She gasped in fake horror. "You take *all* the new kids in town out for barbecue? And here I was thinking I was special."

His eyes flicked to hers, the gold glints flaring as they connected, then he turned back to the road. *Uh-oh.* She'd possibly gone a bit OTT on the buddy-buddy thing.

He finally spoke. "Only the extra-talented ones who get caught in the rain."

A warm swirl of relief and something else a whole lot saucier twirled through her. *He thought she was talented.* She knew she was talented, but to hear it from Ty felt special. He didn't strike her as a doling out compliments kind of guy. She gave a silent cheer whilst trying her very best to keep her grin contained.

"Why don't you pick a channel?" Ty turned the radio on again.

"You go ahead. Your car. Your tunes."

"No, honestly…"

Ty's voice was laced with that dry humor she was beginning to get used to.

"If Stella hasn't told you already, she will no doubt volunteer the information that I have a tendency to get stuck in my ways."

He gave his jaw a scrub, as if considering whether or not to plump for a bit of spontaneity. He gave a solid nod. Decided.

"Why don't you liven things up? Pick something *you'd* listen to in *your* car."

Now she felt stupid. If he had a girlfriend surely she wouldn't choose kids' radio? Not if she wanted to get a ring on her finger, she wouldn't. But if she was sure of anything about Ty it was that if you wanted him you got a package deal. Any man who bought a bright orange car and listened to penguin songs was a devoted daddy.

She thought of the possibly imaginary girlfriend doing Lulu's hair. Helping her into her jim-jams at night. Reading her a chapter or two of

Pippi before turning out the light with a kiss and a murmured, "Sweet dreams." Then she forced herself to stop.

Could loving someone else's child feel the same as loving one of her own?

She looked at Ty's striking profile. He was all strong-jawed, five o'clock shadowed and cheekbone-tastic. His hair was too short to give her the completely insane excuse to brush some of it away from his eyes, but it was tempting.

Who was she kidding? Everything about Ty Sawyer was tempting. She was already wondering about loving a child she'd never met, for heaven's sake!

She turned to look out the window and fuzzed her lips. Falling for him was utterly ridiculous. A pipe dream. Up until now her love life had pretty much consisted of just that. Pipe dreams and delusion juice.

Love had been conditional in her family. Entirely merit-based. *Behave impeccably. Be the captain of the team. Be the best in your class.* It was all she knew. Work and work and prove her worth and still the cuddles from her mother were nothing to look forward to. They were of the weird patting variety that made her feel as if her mother was only doing it because she'd read about it in a manual. And hugs from her father…? Non-existent.

"Go on. Pick a channel, Kirri."

Kirri snapped out of her fug and scanned along the digital options until she landed on a pop music channel.

Ty arched an eyebrow but kept his eyes on the road. "Is this what you listen to back home?"

"It's my guilty pleasure." She sang a few bars, did a couple of silly hand-moves, then sat back in the seat and hummed along until the song ended and another began.

Once again silence fell between them, but this time it felt more...*alive*. Electric, even. The kind of electricity that hummed between two people who were attracted to each other. A turbo-charged frustration.

Half of her wanted to scream, *Pull over now*, jump him and make crazy spontaneous love. The other half wanted to shout at him for being so damn quiet.

Shouldn't he be giving her helpful cues about working at Piedmont? Or, more pressingly, about his daughter? Little pointers about what she was like. Things she liked to talk about. Favorite unicorn. Stuffed toy. Whether or not he was single and why he wasn't spelling out what the arrangements were with his daughter's mom. That sort of thing.

But, no. Just the odd glance that sent her belly into lava lamp mode.

After a few more songs he put on the indicator and left the freeway. "We're just a couple of minutes away now."

"How is your daughter getting there?"

"Oh, my sisters are bringing her. Or my parents. I can't remember. One of them."

Kirri gave a double-take. "You invited your family?"

Hilarious. She'd heard of inviting wingmen along, or at least arranging to get a tactically timed phone call ten minutes in, or in her case faking a page—but inviting his whole family along? That was a new one on her. Then again, perhaps it was genius. Adult buffers right there on site if she went all mealy-mouthed on herself and couldn't talk.

"My parents and my two older sisters will be there. The two younger ones are busy."

"One boy growing up with four sisters? It's a wonder your car isn't pink."

He shot her a glance. "Don't you dare say something like that in front of them."

She gave him a *try me* face.

"Honestly. There is nothing they will not try once a seed is planted. You'll see."

A few minutes later she did.

Ty's family were absolutely wonderful. His parents and his older sisters were indeed there. No girlfriend, fiancée or "family friend". And then there was Lulu. Six years old, the spit of her father and absolutely charming. Lulu Sawyer was officially the first child between two and eighteen to bust Kirri's I-can't-talk-to-you record.

She had a thousand questions about Australia and then some.

"And it's like summer at Christmas?"

"It isn't just *like* summer—it *is* summer!"

"So…" Her little button nose crinkled adorably. "What do you eat after you open your presents?"

Her family weren't much for celebrations, so they usually went to a restaurant—"to give your mother a day off in the kitchen." Her father was simply made of largesse.

She squelched the truth and told Lulu about what other, normal people did. "We have exactly what you have. Turkey and all the trimmings. Others have barbecue. Seafood, usually."

"It sounds amazing. Papa, do you think we should go one day?" Lulu beamed up at him and batted her lashes.

Ah. *Now* she knew why their car was orange.

Ty gave a vague nod, then suddenly became intent on plucking everyone a napkin out of the silver holder.

Half an hour later Kirri was seeing sides of Ty she wouldn't have believed existed. One of America's most innovative surgeons by day, adoring father and much loved son by night. She felt like she was in a sitcom. The really good kind that you wished would never ever end.

The Sawyers were the type of bonkers family she had always dreamed about being a part of. Everyone talked over each other, laughed with each other and very clearly loved one another, despite their different personalities.

Ty was dipping in and out of his role as the strong, silent type, as well as laughing and joking along with his family. But whenever his gaze crept her way it was with all-penetrating looks she was finding harder and harder to read.

She would have thought the sparky hits of connection they'd experienced in the car would disappear once Ty's family absorbed them into the huge booth at Chuck's, but no. They just got sparkier.

"Pass the butter, please."

Zing!

"Would you mind handing the hot sauce over?"

Fizz.

Frisson-laced reminders of that very first time they'd literally crossed paths. Fireworks went off each time their eyes met. Scary, exciting and utterly captivating. He didn't even have to look at her for her tummy to go all flip-floppy with pleasure.

She glanced over and caught Lulu beaming up at him. She bumped the tip of her index finger against his nose in a gesture that clearly meant *I love you, Papa.*

And from the soft smile he unleashed when he tousled her dark hair and gave her a little half-squeeze Kirri instinctively knew it was his way of saying *I love you, too, Lulu. With all my heart.*

It was the type of bond nothing and no one could ever break. It was the type of love she ached for.

Kirri looked away and focused on Ty's parents—Marina and Henry. They were having a spirited conversation about a local baseball team. In their early seventies, she couldn't imagine a more charming couple. Gracious, fun-loving and completely relaxed. They were, in short, the complete opposite of her own parents.

Before she could stop herself she blurted, "Thank you so much for including me on your night out. This is my first proper Southern meal since I've arrived."

Ty's mother's hands flew to her chest as she gasped. "Well, that's just terrible. Henry? Did you hear that? This poor girl's been here all weekend and not had a proper meal." She clucked and wagged her finger at her son. "Ty, you shoulda told us you had a special guest. We would've made a proper fuss over her."

"She's not spe—"

Kirri bit back a pained grin as Ty all but stuffed his actual foot into his mouth.

"Ty!" His mother swatted at him. "Manners!"

His sisters tsked and his father threw him a questioning look.

They all knew where that sentence had been going.

She's not special.

It was a sentiment that shot her straight back to the way her father had made her feel as he'd goaded Lucius on to higher and higher academic success. Sidelined. Unworthy. Hungry for approval she knew she'd never get. Little wonder, considering her father was straight out of the nineteen-fifties *Distant Father Handbook*. Sexist, not entirely politically correct, and utterly driven to make her brother a "proper man" by tearing him down bit by bit and then sitting back to watch as Lucius gathered the pieces and tried to put himself together again.

"And here's the first of it, Dr. Sawyer."

A server appeared, a big smile on his face, his arms weighted with two platters laden with unctuous looking ribs.

Saved by the barbecue!

The Sawyer family applauded their approval as the server slipped an enormous slab of ribs on the table. Everyone except for Ty. He was still beating himself up about that stupid comment.

She's not special.

Of course Kirri was special. Talented, inquisitive, fun-loving and utterly beautiful, to name just a few reasons.

Special enough to take a risk with his heart?

He grabbed a rib and let the flavor explosion drown out that particular line of thinking. He was happy as he was. Forward-thinking, groundbreaking surgeon at work—steady, reliable, chino-wearing dad the rest of the time. It was Stella's fault for planting that ridiculous seed about having an affair. He checked that thought, too. It wasn't Stella's fault. It was his for giving it air.

"Sure that's enough for you, honey? You're our guest and we want to make sure you feel real special."

Ty's sister Patsy sent him a pointed look as she reached for one of the ribs herself. She was the eldest of his two older sisters, both as warm and welcoming as the next. He'd stupidly been hoping they would do what they normally did whenever they met a single woman—talk about all of the men they could set her up with. But, no. They just kept talking about how fabulous Ty was when he wasn't sticking his foot in it. As if they were in some sort of conspiracy with Stella.

Did everyone want him to start dating? Or did everyone want him to date Kirri?

"This is amazing," Kirri said, a bit of sauce trickling down her wrist. "I don't know if I'll *ever* have enough."

At just that moment she stuck out her tongue to lick the sauce off. Her eyes met Ty's and the statement took on a whole new meaning. Hope, fear, wonder and a thousand more emotions were reflected back at him. What shone through most brightly was that neither of them was on familiar territory and that both of them were feeling the same thing: curiosity…

An energy charge shot straight down to his bootstraps. Stella was right. His sisters were right. It *was* time to take a risk, because for the first time since Gemma had died the *person* was right.

Kirri was completely different from Gemma, but he didn't need to see a grief counsellor to know that searching for the same type of woman to replace his dearly departed wife would only end in tears. How could a man replace his childhood sweetheart? He couldn't. But perhaps he could find it in his heart to love someone completely new. Someone like Kirri.

For the next six weeks, anyway.

Kirri blinked and all the questions in those blue eyes of hers were replaced with a light, bright smile.

Perhaps a fun fling was exactly what the doctor ordered. What was the worst that could happen? She'd say no, they'd get on with their jobs and then she'd go back to Australia? Fine. Then he could slip back into the status quo and go on for another five years without anyone pushing him to leave his comfort zone.

Mind you, if his sisters didn't stop discussing what a heathen he was, the possibility of an actual date might not be an option. He looked across as Kirri's grin widened and his sisters batted comments back and forth.

"Who raised you? A wolf?"

"Don't insult Mama. It's Ty who's the heathen."

"Kirri is a treasure. He's been downright rude, not introducing her to us till now."

"I bet it wasn't even his idea. Was Stella the one who knocked some sense into you?"

"I'll bet it was Winny and Reba."

He knew protesting would only add fuel to the fire. Growing up with four sisters had taught him as much.

Kirri was openly laughing now. "Winny and Reba? Who are they?" She took another piece of corn on the cob from the diminishing pile.

"They're Ty's younger sisters," Ty's father explained for him, seeing as his mouth was full of food. "They're at the local park, watching a couple of our grandkids' baseball games along with their own children. How about you and your family? Is it as big and boisterous as ours?"

Shards of something Ty couldn't put his finger on lanced through Kirri's eyes.

"Nope! It's just me and my brother. We're so busy with work I imagine we'd be pretty terrible at the whole traditional family thing."

"Oh, I doubt that," Henry said. "One glimpse into the eyes of your own child and it's instant love. That kind of love runs deep."

"I'm sure it must."

Kirri flashed another one of those quick smiles of hers that didn't quite light up her eyes, then began to rearrange the food on her plate, nodding and listening politely as his father went on to detail all the aunts and uncles who were also involved in the children's lives. And cousins. There were scores of them.

For heaven's sake… Why were they unfurling the family tree? It was obvious the woman didn't have a big family like theirs. And the more his parents went on about it, the more Ty felt as if they were rubbing salt into a raw wound.

Before he had a chance to cut in, his sister Tammy asked, "Is the family you *do* have as nuts as ours?"

"We definitely don't have traditions like this," Kirri said, her voice a bit too bright, her smile slightly frozen. She gave her head a little shake, then swiftly changed the subject. "Did *you* not have a baseball game today, Lulu?"

His daughter shook her head and beamed up at Ty. "No, ma'am. I never let anything get in the way of barbecue and bowling night."

Ty smiled and gave her a squeeze. He dreaded the day that would change. But, as he'd seen with his older sisters' children, change was inevitable. His little firecracker would discover sport, drama club or—God forbid—boys. There would come a day when she went off to college. Led a life of her own. Then he really would be on his own.

"The barbecue is definitely worth leaving the office for," Kirri said, clearly more at ease now they were off the topic of happy families. "But I've never been bowling, so be gentle on me."

His mother jumped in. "Well, thank goodness my boy's finally learnt some manners and got you out of that stuffy condo of yours."

Ty shot Kirri a quick apologetic grimace. She gave him a soft smile in return. And if ever there was a way of saying *you're forgiven* that smile was it. Pure gold dust.

His mother was on a roll. "If we'd known you were here over the weekend we would've had you over for roast chicken or pie. Fattened you up." She gave Kirri a quick once-over and clicked her tongue. "Don't they feed you right over there in Australia? So willowy!" She said it with a splash of good-humored envy rather than as a chastisement.

Kirri laughed. "They do," she said, then admitted, "But this is probably the first full meal I've had in months." She held up her hands before everyone could pile in and chastise her. "Back home I work late most nights, so it means I'm not that great a cook."

"What about your mama? Didn't she teach you the basics?"

Kirri's eyes flicked to Ty's. Before her smile and laughter took over he saw what no one else did. His suspicions were right. She hadn't had a happy childhood. And, no. No one had taught her the basics.

"I get by. Nothing a frozen burrito and a microwave can't fix."

"Oh, well, that won't do." Marina Sawyer fixed her steely dark eyes on Ty. "Son? You're to bring this young woman over next time you release her from that clinic of yours and we will have a cooking lesson. Several, if there's time. One every weekend."

She wasn't giving Ty a choice. He shook his head and grinned. If Kirri didn't watch herself his parents would be signing adoption papers by the time her tenure was over. Which wouldn't exactly jive with the whole *why not have a fling with her?* idea—but he was still on the fence about that one, so…

"Very well, then," Marina said decisively. "I recommend we start with peach pie this Saturday. That way we can have it Sunday after church, when Kirri joins us for family lunch."

Ty didn't bother to protest. Not so much because there wasn't any point but because he loved seeing the spark of joy light up in Kirri's eyes.

CHAPTER FIVE

KIRRI'S FIRST INSTINCT had been to protest, but one look at Ty's mother and she'd known Marina wouldn't hear otherwise.

"Don't bother," Ty said to her warmly. "There's no point in resisting. I'll pick you up on Saturday morning."

The look he gave her was entirely different from anything she'd seen from him before. It said, *I've got your back.* It said, *I saw your sadness.* The insight was humbling. Intimate, almost. As if he knew her better than she knew herself.

The man was like a kaleidoscope. Perfectly wonderful one minute, cool and reserved the next, and then, in the blink of an eye, kinder than she could have ever imagined.

"Right, then. That's settled. Now, let's tackle the rest of this food, shall we?" Marina said with a bright smile.

No one dared disagree. They collectively piled in as more baskets and trays appeared at their booth. Biscuits, of course. So fluffy and buttery Kirri could have eaten a dozen. Collared greens. Beans. Coleslaw. And an endless stream of ribs.

It was clear from the familiarity of the wait-staff that Ty hadn't been lying when he said he came here every week. His daughter even had her picture on the wall, from what must have been her fifth birthday, if the candle count was anything to go by.

Kirri ate and smiled and soaked it all up. She'd done a lot in her life but she had never had a happy, talkative, family meal like this. Ty's family were exactly the type she'd dreamt of growing up in. Rambunctious, non-judgmental. *Loving.*

She crushed the thought with terse pragmatism. *You didn't grow up in a family like that. Move on.*

Marina's heritage was, as Kirri had thought of her son, Latin American. She'd passed on her pitch-black hair to all of her children, and as a born-and-bred Georgia girl sounded every bit as southern as Ty did.

Well, Ty's accent was a lot like warm caramel and it did funny things to her tummy…so perhaps a bit different.

Marina was a third-generation Costa Rican, whose grandparents had come over to study English Literature at college and had ended up being asked to stay on as teachers. It was a tradition that seemed to have trickled down the family in a not altogether linear way. Ty's mom had taught biology. One of his sisters taught history.

"Gemma did, too, of course," Ty's mother said.

"Gemma? Is she another one of your daughters?"

Marina's voice dropped in volume as she checked that Ty was still busily discussing the finer points of doing his daughter's hair properly, after a lecture from his sister Patsy. Fishtail, apparently, was best.

"Oh, honey, I thought you knew… Gemma was Ty's wife."

Kirri's tummy lurched. So he *did* have a wife.

"She passed just over five years ago now."

Her breath froze in her throat. *Ty was a widower.* The thought hadn't even occurred to her. And just like that her heart split wide open for the man.

"Cancer," Marina whispered. "She put treatment on hold to have Lulu, here, but a year after she was born it got the better of her."

She popped on a bright smile and offered Kirri a fresh set of napkins, which she took as a sign that Ty was paying attention to them again.

She picked up a rib and began to eat, because it was all she could do not to throw herself across the table, grab Ty's hands in hers and say, *I get why we're connected now. We both know loss. Heartbreaking, bone-deep, soul-destroying loss.*

It made sense. The reason they clicked and sparred. Pain knew pain. Love recognized love. Advance and retreat, then try again. It was how they survived. It was how she hoped to gain the courage to stop herself from retreating and fill that aching void in her heart one day. The void she was so desperately trying to fill with her pioneering inventions.

Could she ever have room in her life for both?

As if reading her mind, Ty gave her a silent nod. He *saw* her. He saw her more than anyone ever had. And instead of making her feel vulnerable, it filled her heart with peace.

A while later Ty's father knocked his hand on the checkered-clothed table to get their attention. "C'mon, everybody. Finish up. We'll have dessert at the ice cream parlor down at the alley."

Kirri smiled at him. Henry was a tall silver-haired gentleman who had the same lean, athletic physique as his son. He ran a corner shop in exactly the same neighborhood he'd grown up in—Hank's. Which had been his father's name before it had been his own. Kirri really liked him. She liked all of them, if she was being honest.

She let her gaze slide once again toward Ty, who was smiling at his daughter as she devoured the remains of her potato salad.

Ty was a widower.

The news had properly rattled her.

She knew people's deepest traumas shaped them. However much she'd love to avoid the fact that she was trying to develop an artificial womb because she didn't have one, she couldn't. She tried on a daily basis, but her research was torture sometimes. The plain truth was that even if she did make that all-important breakthrough it wasn't as if she'd suddenly have a husband and two-point-four children.

Had Ty's loss affected his relationship with medicine? Was it the reason he was so forward-thinking in the OR? Her work was meant to help women experience the joy she knew she could never have. Was he trying to do the same?

He obviously hadn't remarried. So he'd clearly loved Gemma deeply. That or, like her, he'd buried himself in his work. Work that made him face his worst fears every single day. Saving women and the babies they were carrying from possible death. He must regularly operate on women who had discovered they had cancer when they were pregnant. Did it give him joy to know he'd saved lives or was it a daily reminder of the woman he'd never hold in his arms again?

She forced her thoughts away from unraveling a widower's emotional trauma and focused on Ty's family as their banter continued to fly about the table as freely as air. They emptied the final dishes, joshed, joked and teased about enormous appetites and expanding waistlines, but all of it was loving.

There was none of the bite that usually accompanied her own family's dinner table banter. If you could call the conversation the few times they'd all eaten together and actually spoken "banter". No doubt about it. Her family was definitely...*trickier*.

She and Lucius were her parents' only children. Their father was a highly sought-after neurosurgeon and had always been extremely demanding of them in those rare hours he'd spent at home. Demanding of Lucius, anyway.

Her old pops—something she wouldn't ever dream of calling her father to his face—definitely belonged to another era. In his book men had jobs and women had children. Their mother had been a nurse when she'd met their father, and had given it all up to raise their family, but parenting hadn't brought her the joy it brought so many women. As such, she disappeared into books for days at a time, diving into other people's worlds for a bit of escape from her own.

After he'd found out Kirri couldn't have children, her father had pretty much left her to her own devices. Something she was pretty sure Lucius would've loved for himself. There wasn't a single thing he'd done during their childhood that had gone unnoticed. As such, he still rode himself pretty hard. She wondered what he'd have been like if he'd grown up with easygoing parents like Ty's. Happy?

Hmm… She wasn't sure Lucius was the sort who'd ever be happy. Not with his perfectionist drive.

As they prepared to leave the table Marina cleared her throat and nudged her son. "Isn't there anything you'd like to say to our special guest, honey? Something about not inviting her over earlier?"

Ty's exasperated smile for his mother was hilarious. The one he threw *her* made butterflies take flight.

"I apologize for not inviting you over earlier. I humbly beg your pardon."

Swoon!

"It's fine." She waved off his apology and his mother at long last seemed satisfied. "I was jet-lagged and I had a lot of studying to do. I can't believe how many research projects they're doing at Piedmont. It's really impressive. Besides…" She couldn't seem to get her mouth to stop talking. "He gave me his umbrella."

A round of confused looks turned her way.

"It was raining when we first met. He hit me and—"

"He *hit* you?"

"No! No, no—not like that. We were just— We ran into each other, and it was raining, and he gave me his umbrella."

It had been one of the most spontaneously kind things anyone had ever done for her.

His sisters nodded approvingly as they inched out of the booth with Lulu, to go to the ladies' room and wash all the barbecue sauce off their hands.

Both of Ty's parents turned to their son and his father smiled. "He's a good 'un, our boy. Definitely the brainbox of the family. You must be, too, if they flew you all the way over from Australia. Very special indeed."

She saw Ty feign interest in an invisible stain on his shirt to cover up this new variety of embarrassment. Being spoken about as if they were at a parents' meeting or about to go to prom.

It was kind of adorable. A privilege, really, to see this version of him. She felt as if, with his family's help, she'd unearthed an entirely different human being. Perhaps this was why Stella had urged him into having barbecue with her. A chance to show her the man behind the surgical mask.

"You'll have to tell us all about what it is you're researching when we get to the bowling alley," Henry's dad went on.

She smiled and nodded. She'd become good at that. Explaining her desire to help expectant women while leaving out the part about how she hoped it would fill the emotional void in her own soul.

She had a little speech. A brief but impassioned number she'd curated to assure people that she wasn't playing God, that she was simply helping the preemies who struggled to have a proper chance of survival. She often gave it, then ran off to the ladies' room to have a quick weep, a swift face-wash, before returning with a spark in her eye and a smile on her face that didn't let anyone know her heart had just broken all over again.

She wondered if there would be a day when it would ever stop breaking.

Lulu skipped out of the restroom with her aunties in tow and waved when she saw Kirri. Poor little thing. Losing her mother before she'd even had a chance to get to know her.

Kirri's throat grew thick with emotion, then suddenly she realized Ty's parents were still waiting for an answer. "I'm over the moon to be given this opportunity to carry on with my research. And I'd be more than happy to tell you all about it."

Against her better judgement Kirri looked at Ty. Their eyes caught and meshed. That warm, fuzzy feeling that had been working its way through her bloodstream all night flared again.

Ty reached out and with the pad of his thumb wiped something off the corner of her mouth.

"Sauce," he said, his tongue dipping out to swipe a little left on his own full mouth.

Oh, mercy. This was going to be a long night.

Ty sensed Stella's arrival in the staff kitchen before she spoke. He took his time pouring his coffee, giving it a stir, wiping up the ring on the counter. He knew what was lying in wait. An interrogation.

"So!" She pounced the minute he turned round. "How was it?"

"Barbecue at Chuck's is always good. You know that." He took a sip of his coffee, feigning pure naiveté.

"Dr. Sawyer, you know damn straight I'm not talking about Chuck's."

He laughed. Stella wasn't normally this forthright, so it must have taken all her reserves of patience to wait until this morning to get a full report.

"It was lovely."

"Good. Lovely's good. And did your guest enjoy Chuck's?" Stella blocked the doorway so Ty couldn't get out.

"Very much."

"And did the two of you enjoy your time together?"

"Lulu and I had a ball."

Lulu had actually really taken to Kirri. She'd been a bit shy at first, as she often was with new folk, but once she'd heard Kirri's accent she had suddenly overflowed with questions. She'd even thrown her arms round her waist at the end of the bowling for a spontaneous farewell hug. He might have been wrong, but when Kirri had swept Lulu's hair away from her eyes and wished her goodnight he'd thought her eyes had gone a bit glassy.

He'd never admit it, but his had, too. Up until that moment he'd never imagined his daughter loving another woman as a mother figure. But the way they'd looked at each other... A whole new level of conflict had churned up in him in that instant.

He was an adult. He could look after his own feelings. But not everyone was up to loving a man whose number one priority was his little girl, and he was damned if anyone was going to break his little girl's heart. Least of all a woman whose life was on the other side of the world.

"Dr. Tyson Sawyer," Stella chided. "You know darn straight I wasn't talking about you and Lulu. Though do give that precious little girl of yours a kiss from me. It's been too long." She fixed him with a stern mama bear look. "I was talking about Kirri."

Ty tried to inch his way past her.

"Uh-uh. Not until I hear whether or not you finally offered that poor girl some proper hospitality. And you know what I'm saying by *hospitality*." She dropped a none-too-subtle wink.

Ty frowned. Talking about his sex-life with Stella was about as weird as it was discussing it with his mother. Something he never wanted to do.

He set the record straight sharpish. "We had a nice time. At least she said so when she got in her cab after bowling."

Stella looked appalled. "You didn't drive her back?"

"Well, no. Lulu needed to get to bed, and Patsy and Tammy were going the other way—"

Stella cut him off. "Wait a minute. Are you telling me you invited your *sisters* along? Oh, Ty…"

Before he could protest that he had hardly set out to woo Kirri, Stella continued.

"Tell me you didn't bring your parents along, too?"

She crossed her arms, clucking her dismay when he said yes.

"So let me get this straight. You bring one of the most beautiful women to ever cross our threshold to barbecue, with practically your whole family, and then you stuff her in a cab at the end of the night without so much as a 'welcome to Georgia' kiss? Son, your wooing skills are *rusty*." She tsked her disappointment.

The last time he'd asked someone out formally had been when he'd asked Gemma to prom, and they'd already been dating for a year, so… "I guess you *could* say I'm out of practice."

A softness hit Stella's features. "I know, Ty. But you like this girl." She leant in. "In all honesty, I'm proud of you. I didn't think you'd actually go through with it."

"Why?"

She shrugged, checked behind him to make sure there was no one around. "I just thought you might be too stuck in your ways since you lost Gemma."

"I don't think these types of things come with timelines."

Courtesy of his work, he'd met more than enough men in his shoes, and every single one of them had dealt with their loss differently. Married the nanny. Never remarried. Married someone they met on an internet dating site. Devoted themselves to their children. The list went on.

"No, they don't." Stella stepped to the side so he could pass. "But mark my words. When you get a second chance at finding something wonderful you better reach out and take it."

* * *

After checking there weren't any emergency medical helicopters due, Kirri pushed through the door to the roof and tilted her head up to the sun.

She'd hit a snag in her research and needed a bit of a breather to clear her mind. It was the type of snag that served as a blunt reminder that the clock was ticking. Six weeks had sounded like ages when she'd jumped on the plane a few days ago. A glut of time.

No hovering big brother, wondering when she was going to get back into surgery. No surgical patients to pull at her heartstrings. Just six long, glorious weeks to deep-dive into the world of her baby grow bag.

Today the time limit loomed with terrifying proximity.

Her phone buzzed in her pocket. She answered it without looking, wincing when she heard her brother's not so dulcet tones.

"When are you coming back?"

"Nice to hear from you, too, brother dear," Kirri snapped.

Why couldn't he be more like Ty was with his sisters? Supportive. Loving.

"When are you coming back?"

"I told you. End of June."

"You'll be too late."

Her heart skipped a beat. "For what?"

"We're putting the 3D ultrasound into the operating theater."

Her shoulders dropped from her ears. *Oh.* So he had bought it after all. It was about as close to *I miss you, please come home* as she'd get from her big brother.

She'd trialed the device before she'd left and done a proper sales pitch for Lucius. He'd done the usual. Leaned against the counter in her lab— he wasn't much of a sitter—stared at her, arms crossed, a perfect poker face giving absolutely nothing away. Normally she was used to it. That time it had infuriated her.

A 3D ultrasound would give them a fast, simple and remarkably detailed way to comprehensively evaluate a patient's uterus. What on earth was there to think about? It wasn't as if the clinic was short on cash.

He'd closed their meeting with a request for her to clear out her lab within the week and "get back to some proper work."

That afternoon she'd received Ty's email about the research exchange. One trip to the embassy, two days of mad phone calls later, she'd been packed and ready to go.

She reminded herself of this before she reached out and grabbed the carrot Lucius was dangling in front of her now.

"I've still got five more weeks here. Five and half, really."

Lucius exploded. "What exactly are you trying to prove, Kirri? That just because some other clinic on the other side of the world is blowing money around like confetti you're going to win the Nobel? You're not. What you're doing is too big for you. You need a team. A university's backing. Along with a hospital, a biochemical lab and a proper human study—which will take decades to organize. Maybe longer. You'll have to fight ethics board after ethics board. Politicians. Religious leaders. What is the point of wasting all of this time when you could be helping women here and now? In *Sydney.*"

Tears stung the back of her throat like razors. He definitely knew how to stick the knife in. So much for *I miss you. Please come home. I've bought a new expensive toy for you to play with.*

She wanted to scream at him. Tell him he was wrong. Ask him to offer her the type of support they'd both craved from their father—unconditional. But no words came out.

"Right. Here's the way it's going to go," said Lucius. "You get yourself together. Get on a plane. And come back home."

"And what if I don't? I made a commitment to these people."

"You made a commitment to *me*! And you've

broken it." He huffed out a sigh, then tried a more conciliatory tone. "Let's put it this way, Kirri. Your job here is to be a surgeon. And because I don't want you embarrassing Harborside I'll let you see out this ridiculous exercise of yours."

"*Let* me? Instead of what?" she snapped.

"Firing you for insubordination."

Kirri's heart leapt to her throat. Lucius was right. She'd taken advantage of the fact that they were family. If anyone else on their staff had done this they would've been served their walking papers on ice the second they'd stepped on the plane.

Lucius continued. "Top tip? Spend your time there wisely."

"I *am*."

"I'm not talking about the research lab—I'm talking about the operating theater. They're a notch above the rest over there. You could probably learn a few things if you ever pulled your head away from that microscope of yours."

She was sure there was a compliment in there somewhere, but she was hard pressed to find it. Mind you, he hadn't fired her.

She heard him mutter something to someone else. "Gotta go," he clipped. And then the line went dead.

The hot, angry, tears she'd refused to let fall during the phone call streaked down her cheeks.

Being here was meant to be liberating. Instead she felt stuck between the exact same rock and hard place she'd been stuck in back in Sydney.

She wasn't a fool. She knew she was climbing just about the steepest research mountain of impossibility there was. She also knew that her research filled those empty hours between the end of a long surgical day and dawn. She didn't want to get lost in boozed-up nights or empty love affairs. She wanted meaningful content in her life, and right now that was her research.

If she had any sort of confidence in her mothering skills she'd adopt a child of her own. More than one. But the truth was—thanks to a certain ex-boyfriend—she *did* doubt her ability to offer the pure, wholesale love a parent should offer a child.

She swept the tears away to make room for more. He had been right. Her parents had set a horrible example and beyond neonatal surgery she had just one solitary interest. Making preemies' lives more viable. What did she know of sugar and spice and everything nice? Let alone snips and snails and puppy dog tails?

Right, then. If that was what she wanted to do she'd best get on with it.

She pulled a tissue out of her pocket, tidied up her make-up the best she could without a mirror, then headed for the stairwell door.

Just as she was about to open it the door whooshed open and Ty filled the doorway. She wobbled on her chunky heels and, just as he had that very first time, he reached out to steady her. Only this time their gazes locked and held.

She knew in an instant that he saw through her watery smile. Straight through to the pain and anguish that served as her fuel. Anguish she ached to share with someone who could give her some perspective. But *this* someone…? She didn't think so.

Ty was exactly the wrong audience for what she knew in her heart. There was no way she was going to have a breakthrough while she was here.

"Sorry," she eventually managed, wriggling back from his comforting touch. "I was just getting some fresh air to see if I could work through a problem." She huffed out a little laugh. "Usually I go and watch someone else do a surgery, but there wasn't anything on the board so I thought some actual fresh air might be a novel idea."

"Great minds." Ty tapped the side of his forehead. "I often come up here when I need to figuratively see the light." He smiled and looked out to the clear blue Georgia sky.

Kirri did a mental sign of the cross, grateful he was pretending not to notice that she was upset.

He closed the door behind him.

"Sorry, I—I was just going to get back to the lab."

He pulled a fresh handkerchief out of his pocket and handed it to her. "You might want to tidy up your mascara a bit before you go."

Ah. How embarrassing.

"I'm not much good as a mirror," Ty said. "But I am pretty good at listening."

Kirri frowned. She wasn't sure if the one man who made her blood boil for all the right reasons was the best person to pour her heart out to. Then again, he was the one who'd invited her here to do her groundbreaking research, and if she wasn't able to do it then she might as well let him know he should save his money for someone else.

The idea of giving it up hit her with another wave of tears to fight. She sniffled and gave him a weak smile, suddenly hugely relieved to have someone who was there to simply listen. "You sure?"

"Absolutely. There should've been an operation on the board. Mine. I just had to cancel it. So…"

He looked out to the skyline and rubbed his hand through his hair. From the shadows crossing through his eyes she could tell why it had been canceled. Something had gone wrong with the patient and it wouldn't be safe.

She reached out and gave his arm a squeeze. "Tough one?"

He nodded. "Very. We lost the baby."

She nodded her head at a bench someone had put at the far end of the roof. "Want to talk about it?"

He laughed. "Don't go trying to turn the tables on me. I'm the one who's supposed to be listening to *you*. Besides, how many men do you know who like to talk it out?"

She gave a casual shrug. She didn't know any. "The smart ones?"

He laughed and began walking toward the bench. She was going to take that as an *I'll try*.

"It was an intrapericardial teratoma."

Kirri inhaled sharply. "Those are rare."

No surprise things had gone the way they had. A tumor on a foetus's heart was often a death sentence. *Too* often.

"Very." Ty nodded, his hand rubbing the back of his neck again. "And, as you probably know, the best way to get that particular type of tumor out is during the fetal period."

It was the only way, really. If the rapidly growing tumor wasn't treated, it was lethal.

"And there was nothing that could be done?"

He raked his hand through his short hair. "Of course there was. But..." He blew some air through his lips, clearly trying to steady his emotions. "If I'm being clinical, we got the referral too late. We tried to drain away some of the fluid yesterday, to prepare for the surgery, but then the mother developed pre-eclampsia, the baby's tumor wanted to keep on growing, and—" He stopped. There was no need to spell it out.

She knew what that meant. Choosing one life to save another. Kirri's heart ached for him. It was one of those situations utterly beyond anyone's control, but when you knew you could have done something if only you'd had more time… Torture was what it was. Torture because if the planets had aligned correctly you might have been able to save a life.

"I'm so sorry. It sounds like you've just endured a not so perfect storm."

"It's almost cruel to come outside and see the sun is still shining." He looked away and cleared his throat. "Anyway, the mother's safe. In Intensive Care, but alive."

The way he said it came with unspoken words: *I feel like I failed her.*

Words escaped her as she tried to hand him back his handkerchief. He wasn't crying, but she hoped he would see it for what it was—a gesture of kindness. Empathy, even. She knew more than most that nothing made a situation like this better. It was just a fact. Life could be cruel sometimes, and doctors confronted those cruelties on a daily basis. Sometimes you could just get on with it. Other times…? Not so much.

He looked at the mascara-smudged handkerchief and laughed. "No, thanks. That's for you." He patted his pocket. "I've got back-ups. Tricks of the trade." He shook his head and sat down heavily. "It's just so tough to convince someone they're lucky when the baby they've been carrying for twenty-four weeks has just died."

"I don't suppose it would help if I say I'm sure you did the best you could."

He gave her a soft, sad smile. "I think you know the answer to that one."

She did. It didn't matter how much logic you applied to certain cases. Some hit you harder than others. And this had clearly been a sledgehammer.

They sat in silence for a few moments, listening to the hum of traffic drifting up from the streets below.

Abruptly Ty hooked his ankle up onto his knee and turned toward her. "This wasn't meant to be about me. We're up here because of you."

She laughed outright at that. "You weren't meant to find me here at all! I was hiding."

"What? From me?" Ty made a scary face that quickly melted into genuine concern. "We're a team here at Piedmont. I know I didn't make the best of impressions when we first met, and we still haven't had a chance to have a proper sit-down and talk through your work here—"

Kirri cut him off. "Don't. Seriously. We caught each other off guard, that was all."

Their eyes meshed and held. Warmth flooded her belly as butterflies took flight. *Oh, boy.* He'd definitely caught her off guard. In more ways than one.

Her brother's words came back to her loud and clear. *"Make good use of your time there."* She was pretty sure he hadn't meant ogling the boss.

She ran her hand through her hair and twisted it into a quick knot, as if the gesture would contain the riot of emotions she was experiencing. She stared at her hands, then finally admitted, "I feel embarrassed for being up here now. What you've gone through today puts my situation into perspective."

His brow crinkled. "What situation are you in?"

She debated telling him about her brother's phone call, but then decided to follow her heart. "I had a bit of a hitch today with an element of the 3D printing."

She waited for him to throw up his hands, as her brother would have, but no. Nothing. He just crinkled his gorgeous forehead a little bit and nodded, waiting for more.

"Okay. So… As you know, I'm using organ-on-a-chip technology—"

"The baby grow bag? Yes. Gloria told me you like her nickname for it."

"I do." She grinned. "Very much. So, it's kind of hybrid between a grow bag and an actual gel-based organ, but anyway… Your 3D printer is the thing that will help me most at this phase."

"In what way?"

"Well, using a 3D printed organ is a step up from the original grow bag concept."

"Was it literally a bag?"

"Pretty much. Much more technical, obviously, but to all intents and purposes it looked like a large, clear zip-bag. Research teams trialing them are using premature lambs. All above board, and absolutely no harm to the lambs, but I'd prefer not to venture into animal testing."

He nodded. "That was one of the reasons I was excited by your research. We heard about the team in Japan doing some incredible work, but we don't really have the resources here to do that kind of research."

"What you do is amazing," Kirri said with feeling.

She pulled her knee up onto the bench and propped her chin on it so she and Ty were face to face. Talking about this kind of thing charged her like nothing else.

"Organ-on-a-chip technology could change the

face of medical research. Pure scientific advancement for the betterment of everyone. It's groundbreaking stuff. But it's also in its infancy."

"Ha!" Ty gave her knee a poke. "I see what you did there. In its *infancy.*"

They laughed at the silly wordplay, each of them visibly relaxing into nerdy science talk. "Anyway…" Kirri forced herself to be completely honest. "I'm struggling with the hydrodrel."

"The fluid that's meant to act as an artificial placenta?"

"Exactly."

They talked through details for a while. Ty was surprisingly knowledgeable on the subject, and also completely unfazed by what had thrown Kirri into a tailspin.

"Listen…" He gave her shoulder a squeeze. "This all takes time. I hope you're not pressuring yourself to have some sort of earth-shattering breakthrough in the next six weeks?"

She swallowed down a big lump in her throat that said, *That's exactly what I'm doing.*

Ty's hand stayed on her shoulder. "You're here to exchange information with us. Not work yourself to death with worry. We know research takes years. Decades, even."

"Longer sometimes," Kirri said, knowing that

decades was exactly the sort of timeline she was facing.

Their gazes caught again. Fire flashed through her as the gold flecks in his dark eyes flared. The rest of the world seemed to fade away as Ty reached out and ran a finger along her cheek.

"We're here to support you. If you take one small step forward, we'll be thrilled. If you don't…" He gave a small shrug. "These things happen."

Kirri couldn't help herself.

She leant in and kissed him.

It was meant to be a short, thank-you-so-much-you're-amazing kiss, but the second her lips touched his it became something else entirely. A soft, magical connection.

Both of them pulled back before it could become anything more, but already she knew they had the answer to one unspoken question. They were attracted to each other. Big-time.

She briskly stood up, gave her face a quick swipe with the handkerchief, then clapped her hands together. "Well, on that note, I think I'd better get back to work!"

Ty nodded. Didn't move from the bench.

His eyes remained on the space she'd just been in.

Kirri didn't wait for him to say anything. She fled to the lab, vowing she would take that "one small step forward" in the next five weeks if it was the last thing she did.

It was her only choice. Nothing else would keep that kiss from replaying in her mind.

CHAPTER SIX

"Wow. The board looks chock-a-block today."

Kirri's voice swept through Ty's nervous system like warm honey. It had been a mere twenty-four hours since that rooftop kiss and since then he'd been struggling to think of her in an entirely professional manner.

Not that he'd been all that brilliant in the lead-up to it, but finally touching her, tasting her... It had been like uncorking a bottle of champagne. There was no chance of closing it again.

Like right now, for example. His eyes were glued to hers as if his life depended on it. It was her eyes or her legs, and neither one was giving him any respite from the flares of temptation surging through him every time their paths crossed. But, hell's teeth. Not one of his employees had ever worn a skirt that showed so little thigh to such excellent effect.

Or maybe he simply hadn't noticed before. Not the way he noticed Kirri. Her lips, her hair, her

legs, her waist. He'd catch just a glimpse and heat
would arrow straight below his belt buckle.

Kirri, quite simply, lit him up in a way no one
had since Gemma, and if this awkward little exchange was anything to go by he needed to make
a decision about what to do about it. Ignore it?
He'd never been in this scenario before. Or—
perhaps more courageously—maybe agree that
Stella was right? His family, too, if the non-stop
reminders to bring Kirri along on Saturday for
her cooking lesson were anything to go by.

"Dr. Sawyer?" Kirri was looking between him
and the tablet he was carrying. "Everything all
right?"

"Yes, absolutely. Just—"

*Just lost in those sapphire blue eyes of yours
again.*

Something far too intimate to admit when she
was standing crisply before him in a lab coat, all
but saluting him.

She'd taken to calling him Dr. Sawyer ever
since she'd kissed him. As if that would change
the fact he now knew she tasted as sweetly delicate as the light floral perfume she wore. She'd
been all sorts of polite since then, in fact, but
there was nothing either of them could do about
the fact that they'd shared something special.

When she'd kissed him it had been the opposite of a quick peck. They'd exchanged heat and

intention in that kiss. As if the universe had orchestrated the whole thing. Ever since then he'd wanted to pull her to him. Explore, taste, touch. But the part of him that had never said goodbye to his wife was keeping him in this holding pattern he didn't know how to escape.

"Well…" Kirri gave him a curious look, then turned to go. "See you later."

He didn't want her to go. She brought a fresh energy to the surgical unit that charged him as much as it did the rest of the staff.

"Do something about it when lightning strikes."

"It's twin-to-twin transfusion syndrome. But with triplets."

Kirri turned back around, eyebrows raised. "Oh?"

Fewer than two dozen hospitals in the US did this particular surgery. Far fewer in Australia. Only a handful of surgeons would have had the privilege to perform laser surgery on triplets.

"Boys. Stage four. Apparently they've tried some more natural routes. Horizontal rest, nutritional supplements and external laser therapy. But nothing's worked."

Her eyes flicked up to the ceiling as she did a quick calculation of her own, then dropped down to meet his. "Amniotic reductions?"

He nodded. "The patient's regular obstetrician

has tried it all. But the condition's worsened and the triplets are nearly at twenty-five weeks now."

He tapped on his tablet and showed her the latest scan. She stepped in close enough that he could smell that perfume of hers again. Something sweet and fresh. Jasmine and orange blossom? Grapefruit? His fingers flexed then clenched as he resisted the urge to dip down and inhale from that sweet spot at the base of her neck.

"I see..." Her voice had dropped an octave and her eyes had slipped to half-mast, but they remained linked to his. "Any chance you'll lose one of the babies?"

"Not on *my* watch."

Her tongue swept along her lower lip, unleashing a firestorm of response exactly where he didn't need any blood flow. Not at this precise minute anyway.

Talking another surgeon through a patient's history had never felt like flirting before, but this—teasing out the details of the surgery bit by bit, as if describing the way he was going to make love to her later—was ratcheting up the stakes in an entirely different game.

"The mother's being prepped for surgery now."

He continued to stare into her eyes, willing some sort of invitation to come out of his mouth as naturally as the way she'd leant forward and kissed him.

That was the crazy thing about it. It had been both a surprise and yet completely expected. As if it were the only thing they *could* have done. They'd shared something personal. Felt each other's pain. Soothed the other's sorrow with a soft, perfect kiss. It had been as organic as if they'd known one another for years.

"This sort of magic rarely happens twice."

"Would you like to scrub in?"

She tilted her head to the side and gave her lip a bit of a chew. "I was going to grab some lunch from one of the food trucks outside, then head back to the lab…" She flicked her thumb in the direction of the elevators. "Stella says Friday is always a red-letter day for tacos."

He noticed the light shadows under her eyes. Something told him she been sleeping as much as he had. Minimally. A sense of protectiveness flared in him. Here she was on the other side of the world, where she didn't know a soul, pouring herself into her work as if her life depended on it.

If life had taught him anything, it was that every second of every day was precious, and that some of those precious seconds should be spent outside the office.

His family had made that more than clear after Gemma had died. All he'd wanted to do was work. Give all the other mothers a shot at the motherhood his own wife had missed out on. Slowly, but surely his family had pulled his life into balance. It had started with barbecue and bowling. Perhaps that was what Kirri needed. Someone to look out for her. Remind her that non-stop work never gave a person the balance they needed to see the big picture.

"I'll take you out to eat after." He glanced at his watch. "Grandma Poppy's does a mean chicken and waffle plate."

Kirri gave him a funny look. "That sounds like an odd combination."

"It's a don't-knock-it-till-you-try-it combination. C'mon. Scrub in. We're doing it under local anesthetic. It'll take fifteen…thirty minutes, tops."

He was dangling a carrot and she knew it.

That flash of excitement he'd been hoping for lit up her eyes.

"Go on then. Who needs lunch when there are lives to be saved?"

True to his word, in less than an hour Kirri and Ty were outside of the Piedmont Women and Baby Pavilion, in front of a colorfully decorated food truck, waiting for their lunches.

Kirri was still charged with the adrenaline that came from a successful surgery, even though she'd only been an observer. It had been absolutely fascinating—and so quick! Ty's hands were the type that you'd expect from a gifted surgeon. So *capable*.

Capable of doing a whole lot more than surgery, too, if that single touch of his on the roof was anything to go by.

"Are there any plans to do TTTS laparoscopic surgeries at Harborside?" Ty asked.

He took a sip of his lemonade, then leant against the chunky stone columns that fronted the grand entrance to Piedmont Park.

Kirri took a drink of her icy watermelon juice. "This is amazing."

It was a dodge and she knew it. They would have been able to offer precisely the same surgery if she had stayed at home and followed her brother's course of action: surgery only. She'd been offered the chance to train with one of the specialists at a renowned women's hospital in Melbourne, but she'd been so exhausted from her late nights in the lab that she hadn't made the time.

She covered her unease about the decision with a forced nonchalant shrug. "There are a couple of hospitals in Sydney who do it, so we refer patients on. Sometimes their surgeons come to us, but ideally we'd love for all these innovative surgical procedures to be entirely in-house. It's much easier for the patient."

It was a speech she'd given herself again and again that always ended with the same question: Which patients do you want to help? The ones who need you right now? Or the ones you can help in fifty years' time? The need to pick an answer and dedicate herself to it was tearing her in two.

"That's exactly what we feel here at Piedmont."

The passion in Ty's voice spoke volumes. This was his life's work. His calling. Putting A-list surgeons in place to give his patients—both mother and child—the very best chance of survival. He didn't care if he was the surgeon, though obviously he loved it. His main goal was healthy, happy, unharmed mothers and children.

It was a similar remit at the Harborside Fertility and Neonatal Clinic, but in truth the bulk of its renown came from her brother's "Baby Whisperer" status, and as such most of their clients were there for fertility services before moving on to other hospitals once they'd become pregnant. Unless, of course, there were complications. Complications like those she'd tasked herself with sorting out.

Somewhere, buried under a pile of insecurities, she knew she had her own plaudits, but ever since she'd heard about this line of research back in med school she'd decided the only way to bring true validation to herself as an "incomplete woman" was to move artificial uterus research on to the next level.

"Dr. Sawyer!" Grandma Poppy called them over from the shady spot she'd parked the truck in. "C'mon over here, darlin'. I've got your food ready."

Kirri was relieved for the opportunity to change the conversation to food.

"There are some covered picnic tables over there." Ty nodded to a few tables dotted along the edge of a pretty little pond. "Shall we?"

Kirri took her white to-go box from Grandma Poppy. The tangy scent of tomato and spice wafted up to her.

"You'll want to pick up some napkins, too, honey." Grandma Poppy nodded at Ty, who was collecting a few ketchup packets, then leant down and whispered conspiratorially, "Unless you have another way of getting that sauce off your lips."

Kirri flushed deep red.

"Oh, honey. I've seen the way he looks at you." She gave Kirri a naughty wink. "You make sure you eat those wings of yours real messy."

Kirri could only nod, then run away. She silently followed Ty, who mercifully hadn't heard the exchange.

Of *course* she'd thought about kissing him again. It was one of the reasons she'd burnt the midnight oil in the lab last night. If she'd gone to bed without exhaustion to plummet her into a dreamless sleep she knew fantasy would have been only a few easy blinks of the eye away. And that way danger lay.

She gave Ty a sidelong glance. She wondered if "The Rooftop Incident" was seared at the forefront of his mind as well. Kissing him virtually out of the blue! What had she been *thinking*?

Of his lips, obviously. Or, if she was being kinder to herself, of comforting him. Not that it was her normal modus operandi, but she'd been moved by how deeply he had been affected by his patient's loss, and doubly touched by the generosity of his attitude toward her research. Inviting her to his surgery today and then taking her out for lunch were both thoughtful and generous too. Signs of a man who, against the odds, liked to stop and smell the roses.

After she'd had a few bites of her delicious lunch—a basket loaded with spicy chicken wings, mini-waffles and coleslaw—she asked, "Had you done the TTTS before? With triplets?"

"It was a first for me." Ty picked up his enormous fried chicken salad sandwich and eyed it for the best line of attack. "Kind of fun to do it in front of someone who was so appreciative."

"It was amazing. I really should've taken up an offer I had to learn the technique, but..." She held up her hands. "Time. There never seems to be enough of it."

"I hear you." Ty took a thoughtful bite of his sandwich, then asked, "I've been meaning to ask how you manage to maintain a full surgical load in Sydney as well as do your research."

Her mouth wasn't full, but she swallowed anyway. This was precisely the bone of contention she had with her brother.

She took a risk and told him the truth. "I don't, really."

His brow furrowed. "What do you mean?"

"I do surgery during the day and at night and weekends I do my research." She laughed. "If you knew what my 'lab' looked like you'd howl with laughter."

"Try me."

Ty looked like he meant it, so Kirri told him something she would never tell anyone at home because—well, because reputation was everything to the Wests.

"It's an old storage cupboard."

Ty blinked his surprise but said nothing.

Kirri barreled on. "It's not Lucius's fault. He's so busy with the clinic that research in my area isn't really his thing. As you know, he's the king of all things fertility."

"Yes. Amanda, our top delivery nurse, is really looking forward to doing her exchange there."

"She should be. Did you know they've got a way to select embryos with AI now? It's totally amazing. A game-changer in the IVF world."

Ty nodded, took a bite of his pickle, then said, "It sounds as though your research isn't important to Harborside."

Her heart squeezed tight. It really wasn't. But not for the reasons Ty might think. "Yeah, well... I suppose something's got to take priority."

"Why can't they have equal weight? It's your clinic, too, isn't it?"

"Ha! No! Lucius is the driving force with the clinic. I'm just along for the ride."

Ty looked genuinely shocked. "Is that how you see yourself? As a freeloader?"

"My brother definitely does."

She clamped her hand over her mouth. That wasn't news for public consumption. Especially seeing as Lucius was having one of Ty's staff for an exchange in a few months' time.

Ty shook his head. "I can't believe that. Not with your surgical background."

She backtracked. "He's a true champion of my surgical time. But when it comes to my research all Lucius sees is his kid sister bouncing around in cloud cuckoo land."

"I doubt that."

Kirri snorted. "I wouldn't be so sure." She

chewed on her lip for a minute, then said, "He's pulled the plug on it."

Ty stilled for a moment, then asked, "Any particular reason why?"

"He says my goals are unrealistic."

"What *are* your goals?"

To do the impossible. To fill the void that comes from never being able to have a child of my own.

"I want to do surgery half the time and research half the time. But the clinic can't afford that, so I do research on my own time and surgery full-time."

"No breaks?"

"No life to break for," she admitted.

Ty nodded, non-judgmental as ever. He was a very good listener. A part of her wondered if she'd be here if she had actually tried talking to Lucius rather than jumping on the first available plane. The other part knew that the Wests didn't talk. They pushed themselves to excel.

"You know," Ty began, "the reason I go to barbecue and bowling every Tuesday is because my sisters made me."

"No way!" It was difficult to imagine making Ty Sawyer do anything he didn't want to.

"Hand on heart. My sisters can be every bit as overpowering as your brother."

Kirri shook her head in disbelief. "I can't imagine trying to do the same to Lucius. How did they manage it?"

"First of all, my sisters outnumber me," Ty reminded her. "I have to choose my battles tactically."

She let the words settle in her heart. Maybe that was where she'd gone wrong with Lucius. They were both stubborn, and terrible at communicating, so their battles started as flare-ups over tiny things and inevitably ended in stony silences that gnawed on her conscience.

She gave a micro-shrug. "We have our moments, but honestly I'm happy at Harborside."

She wasn't really. Hadn't been for a while. Working for Lucius meant she'd always be the Baby Whisperer's kid sister and now she'd hit a crossroads. It was time to make a decision. Leave Harborside for good to pursue her research, knowing she might fail, or accept what Lucius had said. That she'd make more difference in the here and now in the OR.

It was a huge decision. One she didn't even begin to know how to make.

Kirri gave her head a shake, then said, "Go on—you were saying about your sisters?"

"They saw what I couldn't." His eyes darkened and a muscle in his jaw twitched.

"Which was…?"

"I'd lost perspective on that all-important work-life balance." He cleared his throat, then smiled at her. "Which is why you and I are sitting in the park, in the middle of a work day, having deep fried chicken and syrup-soaked waffles."

Ty took a huge bite of his overflowing sandwich and when he put it down Kirri got the giggles. There was a blob of mayonnaise on his nose and some of Grandma Poppy's Magic Mystery Sauce trickling down his arm.

Kirri hooted with laughter as she handed him the pile of napkins. "We're both going to need a cardiologist after this."

Ty laughed along with her. "Or a nap."

Kirri tipped her head toward the end of the park, where her condo was. "A ten-minute waddle away there's a king-sized bed, lying in wait."

Their eyes caught and synced in a humming electric bond. Her mouth went dry as she realized what she'd done. Invited him to her bed. He must think she was desperate for him. Well, her body definitely was, but that wasn't the point.

A hysteria-edged laugh burbled up and out of her throat along with, "I'm totally kidding!" She swallowed when his eyes stayed glued to hers. "Obviously..." The word came out as a question.

"You do look a bit tired."

Her heart careened around her ribcage. Was he accepting her invitation to bed? She narrowed her eyes. He looked serious. Concerned, actually.

Ah. Not a come-on. Just an observation. She hid the disappointment she hadn't expected to feel.

"It's your fault I want to work all the time." She pointed behind her toward the skyscraper where their offices were. "There are far too many temptations up there."

Ty arched an eyebrow.

Stop using sexy talk when you're describing work, you dill!

Ty's tone was serious. "Don't push yourself too hard. I know the exchange has a time limit, but remember now that you know the team sharing information will be much easier."

Kirri knew her laugh sounded false. "But sharing the 3D printer won't!" She waved off her comment before he could reply. "Honestly. There's nothing for you to worry about. I've just been enjoying playing with your fancy equipment, is all."

"Kirri…" Ty's expression turned completely serious. "I didn't invite you over here to work yourself to death. Yes, the research is important. Everything we do at the clinic is. Life and death sometimes. But there's a balance. Your personal wellbeing is every bit as important as the things you work on."

"Sure." She took a big bite of waffle to stop herself from saying what she really wanted to—

which was that there couldn't be balance in her life. *Ever*.

She had always burnt the candle at both ends. Cracked it in half and burnt it at four ends when she could. It was how she'd been programmed. There was no red light at the end of her work day. Green was the only color that mattered if she wanted to make changes. Be someone who'd made a difference. So she was *go, go, go* all the way.

What did it matter if she was a burnt-out husk at the end of the day? It wasn't like she had a child to go home to like Ty did. Her job was to make sure other expectant parents had a baby to go home to. A child to raise. If she could do that, then she would find some balance.

Ty was looking intently at her, those dark eyes of his impossible to read. Was he trying to figure out if she was worth the investment? A workaholic? Or just plain crazy? It was impossible to tell, so she did what she usually did in these situations—carried on talking until she found herself an out.

"In fact, if it's all right, I'd love to be able to work on the weekend. Is the lab open or do I need special keys?"

His expression shifted, as if he'd made a decision. "I'm afraid you aren't going to be free this weekend."

CHAPTER SEVEN

Ty GLANCED ACROSS at Lulu. She was merrily singing away along with a song about an elephant and trying to teach Kirri the lyrics. Quite unsuccessfully, if the number of corrections were anything to go by.

Lulu was twisted round in her seat so she could face Kirri, who had insisted on sitting in the back of the car when they'd collected her this morning. "No changes on my account," she'd quipped as she'd jumped into the back.

She looked a bit tense and, if he wasn't mistaken, still quite tired. He would put money on the fact she'd stayed late at the lab, despite his popping his head in about six o'clock last night and securing a promise from her that she'd be leaving soon.

An increasingly familiar flare of protectiveness shot through him. Something was driving Kirri's research beyond the obvious. Apart from her brother, she hadn't mentioned much about her

"I'm not?"

"No, ma'am." Ty shook his head and put down the remains of his sandwich. "My mother would never let me hear the end of it if I didn't bring you to your cooking lesson. She's already bought more peaches than you can shake a stick at."

Kirri pinned on a smile. There went her plan to put some space between her and Ty. Then again, if she'd really wanted to do that she wouldn't have scrubbed in on his surgery or be sat here munching on Mama Poppy's finest with him.

"Your mother has got her work cut out for her."

"You're a can't-boil-an-egg type of cook?"

"Can't-boil-water type of cook."

She dragged a fry through a puddle of ketchup, then caught Ty looking a bit more pleased with himself than she might have imagined for someone whose social calendar looked set to be eaten alive by Kirri's inability to cook.

"Are you staying for the lesson?"

His smile broadened. "Wolves couldn't keep me away."

personal life. The few times he'd tried to get her to open up she'd deftly changed the topic. Today he had his secret weapons. His mother and sisters. They could draw blood from a stone.

Not that he was equating Kirri to anything even closely resembling a stone. Far from it. But it pained him to think there was something dark driving her to work the way she did. The type of work they did had to come from a place of joy or it could easily destroy a soul.

"Here we are." Ty pulled his car into the drive of his parents' house, smiling when he saw Kirri's eyes widen. His gut told him bringing her here was a good idea.

"This is beautiful," she whispered, opening the car door and slipping to the ground, her eyes still glued to his parents' colonial-style home.

Lulu, as ever, was already running up onto the porch and through the front door.

"It looks great now," Ty said, unable to keep the pride out of his voice. "But it was definitely a challenge to grow up here."

"What do you mean?" Kirri threw him a look as she waited for him to lock the car and head up the drive to the wide covered porch circling the house.

"When they bought it, it was about as close to a wreck as you can imagine."

"Seriously? And you all moved in straight away?"

He laughed at the memory. "We couldn't wait."

"Why?"

"Before this we lived above Dad's shop in a two-bedroom apartment."

Kirri's hands flew to her chest. "All *seven* of you?"

"Yes, ma'am. My older sisters were in bunk beds, I was in a trundle bed, and Winny and Reba shared a crib. My parents soon decided giving everyone a bit more personal space was a good idea." He smiled up at the house. "They have never shied away from a challenge."

Kirri looked from the house to him, then back at the house. "I'm going to take a wild guess and suggest that you inherited some of that gusto."

Ty smiled. It was the type of compliment people usually reserved for his sisters. "What makes you say that?"

She laughed. "Uh…elite medical practice? First-class facilities? Triumphant surgeries few other doctors would even think about, let alone try? Not just *anyone* could have done all that. It's impressive. Much like this house."

Before he could say he wouldn't have tried to have any of those things if his life plan hadn't been ripped out from under him, Ty's mother appeared on the porch, along with her two middle-aged bloodhounds Pootle and Piggy. His nieces had named them when they were little, and no one had bothered to override their decision.

"C'mon in, you two." She beckoned them to join her. "There's dozens of peaches waiting to be pitted. Crusts to make. Pies to fill. I told the church I'd be bringing half a dozen over for the youth group, so we'd best get cracking."

Kirri shot Ty a triumphant grin. "Like I said—I don't think the apple fell too far from the tree."

Warmth filled his chest as he watched her jog up to the porch, accept his mother's inevitable bear hug, then be ushered into the house along with the dogs. He'd never really thought of himself being like his family before, but he supposed they were all cut from a similar cloth.

His parents embodied everything he hoped he could offer his own daughter. Constancy. Loyalty. Unwavering love. Up until now he'd never thought that his goals could also involve meeting and possibly loving someone new. The hole in his heart made when Gemma had died had become so enormous he simply couldn't imagine the darkness ever becoming light. But perhaps the light had never gone…perhaps it had just been surrounded by darkness and impossible to see.

He went into the kitchen, where his mother was popping a flowery apron on Kirri and setting her up at the kitchen table with an enormous bag of flour and some butter, alongside some sort of kitchen gadget that was going to whiz it all together.

She was like this with everyone, his mother. "Giving my waifs and strays a bit of love," was how she put it. He'd often wondered how she had room in her heart for them all, but looking at Kirri now, and feeling the heat in his own heart, he began to realize that hearts didn't necessarily push things aside to make room for new love. They grew. Expanded to embrace all the love and joy they could.

His mother looked across at him from the counter and said, "I don't know what you're standing there for, son. Come on and join us."

With a smile on his face, he did just that.

Two hours later Kirri had never felt more relaxed or at home than she did here and now in Marina's kitchen. Ty's mother was gracious, patient, kind, and utterly engaged in everything whirling about her.

Dogs. Cats. Grandchildren racing in in their baseball uniforms, asking for one of the huge discs of chocolate chip cookies in a huge old jar. Her husband wandering through, stealing a peach whilst wondering aloud where all the fishing things had got to. Saying he wanted to take Lulu down to the lake, see if they could catch anything.

There were daughters on the phone. Daughters in the house. Daughters picking up and dropping off yet more grandchildren. Ty asking if they minded as he wandered off to do something out in the shed. He was granted permission on condition that he came back once all the peaches had been sliced.

That had been about an hour earlier, and in that time Marina and Kirri had reduced the pile of peaches from enormous to just a few left.

Marina looked out the window and gave a loving cluck. "That boy of mine… He'd live in that shed if there weren't some women in his life to drag him out of it again. His father's just the same."

Kirri nodded. All this was so different from her own family.

As if cued by her lack of response, Marina asked, "How about your own family? They must be missing you, with you being so far away and all. I don't think I could bear it if any of mine upped stakes and moved out of Atlanta, let alone out of the country."

Kirri's laugh sounded far more forlorn than she'd intended.

"You all right, honey? I haven't made you homesick by bringing it up."

"No," Kirri said solidly. "Not in the slightest. If anything…"

"Yes?" Marina handed her a peach. "If anything…?"

"If anything it's made me wistful. Being here with you like this."

"Wistful? What on earth…? Honey, you must be seeing things. This place is a madhouse."

"It's a lot better than silence."

Marina stopped what she was doing and looked Kirri square in the eye. "I can't imagine you growing up in a silent house. You're so full of life yourself."

"Oh…trust me. It was quiet."

Intimidating was what it had been. Family dinners had usually ended up being interrogations for Lucius. Had he passed this exam? Had he got that extra credit? Had he signed up for this club or that club? Activities that would put him in good stead with the best universities.

The answer had always been yes, but none of it had seemed to matter. No matter what, Lucius hadn't been able to satisfy their father. Neither of them had. It was easier, they'd both learned, to study some more or hide away in their rooms with a book. Escape, as their mother did, into someone else's life.

That was what Kirri wanted to do right now. Escape into this life—but for real. Knowing she couldn't twisted her heart so tight she closed her eyes against the pain.

"Are you all right, honey?"

Kirri forced herself to open her eyes, smile and slice up the peach she was holding. "I'm fine."

"I'm sorry if I dredged up some bad memories. But surely you've got some loved ones back home who are missing your beautiful face?"

Again the ache of losing something she'd never had filled Kirri's chest. Her mother had never once told her she was beautiful.

"My family doesn't really work like that. I always hoped that one day I might—" She stopped herself. Dreaming the impossible was almost as crazy as trying to invent the impossible.

"Go on, honey. Finish what you were saying. Everyone's allowed a few hopes and dreams."

Marina's words felt like a warm embrace. "I'd hoped to have a family of my own one day. Like yours. Big and boisterous and a bit crazy."

Marina got up and pulled her into a hug. "You're welcome to be a part of our big family while you're here, sweetheart. There's always room at our table for one more." She held up a finger and wagged it at her before returning to the peaches. "And once you go, don't you dare forget us."

"Not a chance," Kirri said, selecting another peach and getting to work with a gusto she hadn't felt in ages.

The screen door swung open and in walked Ty, carrying a small wooden birdhouse by the tips of his fingers. It was a gorgeous little thing, painted eggshell-blue.

Kirri breathed a soft *ooh*. "Is this what you do in your spare time?"

"Lulu said she wanted one. I know it's a bit late in the nesting season, but there's never any harm in trying, is there? Even if we're a bit late in the game?"

When his eyes hit hers an explosion of connection punched her in the chest. He had been talking about birds, right? She looked away when she noticed Marina's eyes flicking between the pair of them.

"Ty, honey? Why are you holding that birdbox as if it were made of poison?"

"Wet paint," he explained.

Marina pointed toward the door. "Kirri, run and get some newspapers from the back porch, would you, honey?"

Kirri did as she was asked. As she left the room she heard Marina lower her voice and a swift exchange of conversation. A sneaking suspicion told her it was about her.

When she came back in, Marina smiled up at her and said, "It's decided."

"What is?"

"You and Ty are going out to the bowling alley tonight, after supper."

"Oh?"

"Yes. Lulu and her grandfather are going fishing, and of course if she catches anything she's going to have to learn how to clean it and all that. When they get back, the girls want me to bring Lulu over to play with their kids. Tammy's got a pool—her husband does very well in the plumbing trade—and Lulu does *love* to swim. I've got my quilting group to go to, and Ty's father wants to stock-take down at the store, so that just leaves the two of you with nothing to do but twiddle your thumbs. Ty and I did some blue sky thinking just now and we thought it'd be a good idea for Ty to get you brushed up on your bowling before we all meet next Tuesday for barbecue."

Kirri threw a questioning look at Ty. If he showed even the slightest sign of not wanting to go she'd back out faster than he could say *boo*. But his dark eyes twinkled as he glanced at Marina then shrugged at Kirri. His happy, contented face said one thing: *resistance is futile*.

"I think my mother is making a very long-winded attempt at ensuring I ask you out on the date I said I was going to take you on."

What? Date? That had been his plan all along?

"Oh, Ty, you weren't meant to put it like that," Marina scolded, then turned apologetically to

Kirri. "I was trying to make it look more casual, but you looked so sad just now, and whenever I mentioned Ty you brightened up. The pair of you both work so hard, and you haven't had any quality adult time in just about forever, so I thought—"

"Mother!" Ty held up his hands for her to stop, his eyes all crinkled with laugh lines. "I was going to ask her!"

Really? Kirri felt as though she was sixteen all over again. A bit shy, very full of hope, and ridiculously happy.

"Well, you were being a slowpoke, Ty." Marina leant toward Kirri and stage-whispered, "Slow and steady wins the race, but sometimes I question that logic." She turned back to her son. "I'm just looking after Kirri's best interest, is all. And yours. Now, if you *don't* want to go out I'm happy to leave the two of you here with some supper, so you can watch a movie or something. Perhaps Kirri could show you a documentary on Australia?"

"Mama!" Ty was out-and-out laughing now. "We're going out!" He turned to Kirri, his eyes flickering with fun. "That is if you're happy to join me?"

Oh, she was. More than anything she was. But

she seemed utterly tongue-tied and unable to say as much.

Then came the moment their eyes connected. And Ty had his *yes.*

Kirri and Ty handed in their shoes and took the bowling shoes from the teenage clerk.

"Date night?" The lad winked at Ty, then said to Kirri, "Be careful. This guy's a demon on the lanes."

What the—? Was everyone in Atlanta intent on setting the two of them up? Not that Kirri was exactly resisting, but...*the bowling alley clerk*?

Ty rolled his eyes at the boy, then pointed toward their lane. "My mother must've called him."

Kirri whipped around and shot the boy a look. He was already busy chatting up some pretty teenage girls.

She looked back at Ty. "Seriously?"

"No!" Ty laughed. "But I wouldn't put it past her."

He gestured to a chair at the top of lane number twenty-three. She sat down and began to put on the colorful bowling shoes.

"You sure you're up for a night out?" he asked.

"Of course—why?" Insecurity flickered in her eyes.

"It's just been a busy day, is all. Don't want to tire you out."

"You're not. Honestly, the day has been completely energizing."

"Well, hats off to you for surviving the Sawyer Clan. It can get a bit OTT for some."

"Don't apologize. They're a whole lot better than *my* insane family," she said with feeling.

She picked up a bowling ball and threw him a quick smile, but he could see the same flash of hurt that had flared when she spoke of her brother.

If there was one thing his family had never made him feel it was pain. Quite the opposite, in fact. His family were the ones he and Gemma had gone to when they'd been to the obstetrician and then the oncologist for that soul-destroying appointment. His parents and sisters were the ones who'd picked him up off the ground when his wife had been buried. They were the foundation of his existence, and it hurt him to see that Kirri didn't have the same.

He made a feeble stab at offering her a bright side. "I'm sure growing up with your brother wasn't nearly as bad as growing up with four sisters."

"Oh…it wasn't so much my brother that was the problem."

For the first time that night she refused to meet his eye. *Ah. Complicated parents.*

She didn't offer any more details. Instead she

bounced on the balls of her feet, as if testing her bowling shoes for buoyancy.

"Anyway… As you've no doubt gleaned, Lucius comes with his own set of 'interesting.'" She barked out a mirthless laugh. "He probably would've paid cold hard cash—and a lot of it—to have parents as proud of him as yours are of you."

Now, *that* was strange… "I thought Lucius was Australia's number one—?"

"Baby Whisperer," they finished together.

Kirri scrunched up her nose and finally met his gaze. What he saw in those clear blue eyes of hers was a world of complication. Love, sadness, pain.

"He is. But, honestly, I think he'd rather be called anything *but* the Baby Whisperer." She scuffed at the floor with the toe of her shoe. "I hate it, too, to be honest. No one can 'whisper' babies into existence."

She looked like she was going to say something else, then changed her mind and waved it off.

"Anyway. He's amazing at what he does."

She gave her lower lip a grating with her teeth, making her appear utterly vulnerable. It was all Ty could do not to pull her into his arms and tell her it would be all right.

It was what his family had told him again and again after Gemma had gone. *It'll be all right.* But they were just words, and they hadn't changed what had happened. But day by day, month by month, year by year…they had eventually proved to be mostly true.

The sun still rose each morning. His daughter was a blossoming testament to his wife's gentle spirit and his own family's fiery drive to pursue happiness above all. And, of course, there was his work. Work which had unexpectedly led him to Kirri.

As embarrassing as it was to have had his mother ask Kirri out for him, the nudge hadn't been ill-judged.

Sometimes he wondered if he used his grief as a cloak for being plain, old-fashioned chicken. He'd never really had to ask anyone out before. Face rejection. Figure out how to shield his daughter to ensure she was the last one who could be hurt by his inevitable false starts on the dating front. So he'd simply closed the door on all of it.

Until now.

Maybe it was still a cowardly attempt at dating—choosing a woman he knew was going to leave. But…how had Stella put it? A trial run? Maybe she was after something short-term, too. A hot, feverish romance the pair of them could lock up safe as a good memory when their lives returned to normal.

Who wanted normal when you could have sublime?

He pulled on his bowling shoes, keeping a casual eye on Kirri as she eyed up the bowling ball rack. She was a beautiful woman. Even in the awful fluorescent lighting of the bowling alley it was impossible to ignore the effect being near her had on him.

If he was being entirely honest, Kirri was awakening all sorts of feelings in him that he didn't know what to do with. Have a fling and consider himself officially cured of the grief that had shrouded his life in the wake of his wife's death? Or lose control and fall in love only to have to say goodbye.

There was always the other option. Do nothing and stay stuck in the same holding pattern he'd been in for the last five years.

He dismissed the thought. It seemed everyone in his world had long since recognized it was time for a change apart from him. His parents were pushing him toward it, and his sisters. Hell, even Stella at work. And he felt himself become more...*alive*...when he was with Kirri. Something clicked into place there and then. Kirri was definitely the one he should be taking the risk on. Whatever happened it would be worth the fallout.

He watched as she put down the first bowling ball she'd selected, then picked up a sparkly red one instead and gave it a grim nod. As if she planned to use it to blast away the unhappy memories he'd unwittingly brought up. He glanced across to the bar and wondered if he should offer to buy her a beer and sit down and talk instead.

She suddenly jabbed her finger into the air between them. "And don't think just because he's my big brother I'm blowing smoke up his ass or anything. He's a right royal pain and working for him is no walk in the park."

He couldn't help it. He clicked his heels together and saluted. "Yes, ma'am."

He was rewarded with a snort and a giggle that perfectly broke any remaining tension between them.

Ty's chest warmed with a long-forgotten sensation. *Pleasure.* Pleasure at bringing a spark of joy to someone. And not just to any someone. A someone whose arrival had metaphorically crashed into his very set routine and given it a good shake.

Vulnerable and strong. Funny and fierce. What other layers were there to this woman?

Unpeeling them could be one of the most enjoyable things he'd ever done. And there was nothing like a brisk bowling match to literally get the ball rolling.

He gave his hands a quick clap and a rub. "Right! Want to throw a few practice bowls?"

She swept her hand over her bowling ball, then licked her lips. "You sure you're up for playing a maverick like me?"

His eyes stayed glued to her lips as they curved into a teasing smile just ripe for a cheeky kiss.

Instead of breaking the tension that hummed between them, Kirri's sassy approach to bowling only served to heighten them. She threw a few practice runs. All of them pitched straight into the gutter. Ty tried to offer her advice, but each time she leant in to her chosen bowling position he kept going cross-eyed, trying to keep one eye on her technique and the other on the way the fabric of her clothing swept along her curves.

She still had that chic biker girl aesthetic going on. Everything fit her as though it were tailor-made. Her light leather jacket had been casually discarded on a plastic seat by the rack of bowling balls. Figure-hugging jeans with a tactical rip or two swept along her long legs. Her dark auburn hair was free tonight, flowing across her shoulders and down her back to where her waist-skimming T-shirt cinched in then swept out toward her hips.

It was jeans and a T-shirt, really, but on Kirri they oozed attitude and panache. She even made the bowling shoes look cool.

No one's asking you to fall in love or elope... just have fun.

Could he do that after all these years? Just have fun?

He'd married his high school sweetheart.

Loved her until the day she'd died. Just as they'd promised one another at the altar during their white wedding. Longer, even. To this day he'd never known another woman's touch.

But he felt vital and alive in a way he'd never experienced before. It was as if a part of him had physically died along with his wife and an entirely brand new part of him had come to life when Kirri arrived.

It was an entirely different sensation from the way he'd felt with Gemma. Loving her had been as natural as breathing. They'd been through all the important firsts together. Had known each other inside out. This—whatever it was he was feeling now—was more raw. An unrefined, unfettered, uncheckable attraction that felt too dangerous to give freedom to and too serendipitous to let the chance for happiness pass him by.

And just like that a core-deep need to sweep his hands along Kirri's waist, hips, curvy ass and anywhere else she'd let him touch her took hold of him. *He wanted her.*

He strode to her spot beside the bowling ball stand, turned her around and cupped his hands on either side of her face. One look told him she was feeling the exact same thing. An instant need not to be in the bowling alley anymore.

And when their lips touched…?
Fire.

CHAPTER EIGHT

KIRRI WAS HUMMING INSIDE. So much so she didn't think she could bear the tension anymore. So she tried one of her least marketable skills: casual chit-chat.

"This is a nice neighborhood."

Ty glanced at Kirri and nodded. He hadn't said a word the entire twenty-minute drive from the bowling alley. Normally she'd be kind of freaked out by this sort of behavior. A crazy mad snog in the middle of bowling alley and then…mute driving. But in Ty's case it was kind of sexy. Like sitting next to a lion before he decided to pounce. No. A panther. Any sort of sexy beast, really. Because whatever it was, it was making her feel more dangerously desirable than she ever had. Taut with pent-up lust.

She pressed her forehead to the window, enjoying the cool of the glass. It *was* actually a nice neighborhood. Not too different from his parents'. Leafy. Beautiful manicured gardens. Wide inviting porches wreathed with flower baskets offsetting beautiful pastel-colored homes. It screamed *family neighborhood.*

"I know it sounds ridiculous, but I didn't expect to see so many traditional houses so close to the city center. For some reason I thought all the old ones would be out in the countryside. There are loads out in the countryside in Oz. I mean, obviously there are some old buildings in Sydney, but… Anyway. I like your neighborhood."

Kirri cringed. She sounded like an idiot. The handful of intimate liaisons she'd had over the years had been little more than fleeting flares of lust. After the Crusher of Dreams had dumped her cold she'd made sure her emotions remained in check. But this…? This felt different.

What she'd felt when they kissed hadn't been the temporary flicker of a lighter's flame. No, this heat burnt brighter. Stronger. To the point where it was driving her to talk pure nonsense, when all she really wanted to do was flip up the SUV's irritatingly wide armrests and start tearing Ty's clothes off. Not safe driving practice, of course, but…*that kiss!*

She hadn't thought he had it in him. Well, she *had* thought he had it in him—she just hadn't thought he had it in him to give to *her!*

He was reserved. Losing his wife would definitely account for that. And brilliant. He had, after all, recognized the merits of her own research. Not to mention he was an adoring father whose family clearly thought the world of him. They had been the ones to push them out the door to the bowling alley after a scrumptious seafood pasta dinner.

And more than any of that? He'd kissed her as though the rest of the world had faded away and the only thing on this great big blue marble they lived on was the two of them.

Her belly fluttered afresh at the thought.

Yes, she wanted to kiss him, all right. Kiss him and rip off that plaid shirt and those walnut-colored chinos of his so she could see what else he had going on beneath that calm, cool exterior of his.

Or… She slipped her hands along her thighs. Perhaps *he* would take the lead. Start slow. Real slow. Just as slowly as his fingers had slipped along her jawline as millimeter by millimeter he'd lowered his full mouth to hers for one of the most sensual kisses she had ever experienced. It had been an extraordinary combination of tenderness and passion. Far better than the rooftop kiss. It had literally weakened her knees.

A tickling of glittery warmth whispered all the way through to her toes and right back up again, until it took a naughty heated swirl round the magic spot between her thighs.

Before she could travel down memory lane too far, he pulled the car into a driveway in front of a beautiful Victorian house tucked back from the street amongst a nestling of mature oak trees.

"Oh, Ty. It's gorgeous."

His lips tightened for a microsecond. It definitely wasn't the move of a sexy panther about to pounce on his sexy prey.

Then it hit her. This was where he had lived with his wife. It had to be. It was the perfect family home.

The house was two-story, a lush sage-green with white-edged windows, some of which were curved or made of beautiful multi-colored stained glass. There was a sprawling porch dappled with cushioned rocking chairs. It was clearly kept with a loving attention to the details that had no doubt made it shine back in the day when it had been built.

Were they details his wife had put into place?

"It was built in 1891 for a local physician. It even has a turret." Ty spoke mechanically. As if he'd memorized the description the real estate agent had used to lure in buyers.

"How amazing. And…" She hesitated, because she knew what she was going to say would ask more than one question. "How long have you lived here?"

Ty leant forward, looped an arm across the top

of his steering wheel and gave the house a long, hard stare. "Just about five years now."

The way he said it tore at her heart. Five years ago—shortly after his wife had passed.

She knew straight away that she wouldn't be going through that beautiful front door where a stained-glass posy of wildflowers was set into the center of the pale blue window. The same egg-shell color as the birdbox that was sitting in the back of his car.

No. She wouldn't be walking through that door. Not tonight. Perhaps not ever.

The look in Ty's eyes was such a tangle of confusion it obliterated the taut sensual atmosphere that had been buzzing between them. Which was probably just as well. He was her boss. She was here to focus. Not to— Well. Not to do other things.

She tugged up the zip on her leather jacket and pulled her handbag onto her shoulder.

"If it's all right, I think I'd better get a taxi back," she said just as Ty started to say something else.

They false-started a couple more times, stumbling over their words, talking over each other, until Ty finally held up his hands and said, "I think I owe you an apology."

"What for?"

"Kissing you the way I did and then manhandling you into the car."

She actually laughed. "You didn't *manhandle* me. I was a willing participant."

He arced an eyebrow.

"Seriously?" she said. "Number one: if I'd been scared or unhappy we were in the middle of a bowling alley. Help was just a scream away. Number two: you're practically *made* of honor. Any fool can see that." She tapped a third finger. "More to the point, if you had pulled the car into any vacant lot on the way here I would've happily steamed up the windows with you."

The corners of his mouth twitched. Amused or irked? It was difficult to gauge his true feelings. Kirri threw tact to the wayside and decided to do what she always did. Put the facts on the table and see what happened.

"Look. I fancied you from the moment I saw you, and it seems maybe you fancied me a little bit, too. But I'm not a relationship girl, and I doubt you're a fling kind of guy, so it's probably best if we nip this in the bud."

The corners of Ty's mouth tipped down. "It's not you—"

"I know." Kirri waved her hands. She knew the speech because she'd given it enough.

My work is my life. I'm not in the right place

*right now. You deserve someone who can give
you the life you deserve.*

"Why don't we go up onto that porch of yours
and wait for the taxi you're just about to call me?"

At long last that broad, relaxed smile of his
peeled his lips apart. "Compromise?"

"Depends. What kind of compromise?"

"We have a drink on the patio. Talk it out."

"I thought big roughty-toughty men like you
didn't like to talk things out?"

"You think I'm roughty-toughty?"

"You built a birdbox, didn't you?"

He looked up at the house in front of them. "I
rebuilt this house…"

"Well, then. Sounds like we have a good starting point."

"Here you are. Hot tea, as ordered."

Ty handed Kirri the steaming mug, then sat on
the brightly cushioned chair next to her.

"And the taxi?"

"I'm more than happy to drive you home. Remember Lulu's staying at her aunt's, so I'm happy
to be of service."

More time in an enclosed space with her when
he was still buzzing with lust? *What was he thinking?*

Kirri shook her head. "I think going home on
my own would be wise."

Ty nodded, pulled out his phone and tapped a few buttons. "It should be here in forty-five minutes to an hour."

She raised her eyebrows.

"There was a baseball game tonight and traffic's a bit heavy."

"Ah." She stared at her tea as if it were a crystal ball that could magic up a taxi straight away.

They sipped their beverages for a few awkward moments.

She'd been straight up with him, so he might as well do the same with her. "You know that attraction thing you were talking about?"

She nodded as she lifted the mug up to her lips, disguising her expression.

"Well, you were right. It went both ways."

Kirri sat up a bit higher in her chair. "Go on."

There was a playful note to her voice, but he knew it was time for honesty. "I've been wondering from the day we met what it would be like to kiss you."

"You found out the other day on the roof."

"I know. And it made me want more."

"You've got a funny of showing it. Not that I'm all that brilliant at personal relations myself," she added hastily.

He laughed softly, rubbing his thumb along the back of her hand. "I suppose the thing is I haven't wondered anything about kissing anyone in a long, long time."

Kirri nodded, then gave him a nervous grin. "You're very good at it, if you don't mind me saying."

He gave the back of his head a scrub, his eyes traveling the length of the porch as he did so. "Can I be honest with you?"

"Please."

"The truth is, when it comes to you I want to do a whole lot more than kissing. And that's something I haven't done since Gemma passed."

She lifted her eyebrows but said nothing.

"Up until the moment I pulled into the drive my plan was to carry you into the house and tease every thread of fabric off of your body—to do my damnedest to make you feel as hot and bothered as you make *me* feel."

It was a huge admission and, surprisingly, he felt a weight lift off his chest as the words found purchase in another one of Kirri's beautiful smiles.

"What stopped you?"

"Seeing the house."

Kirri gave his hand a soft squeeze but said nothing. She was giving him the time and space to tell his story at his own pace.

"We used to drive past this house all the time, Gemma and I. It was old and crumbling to bits. A lot like my parents' house was when they bought it. Neither of us could bear to see it fall into ruin, so we set our hearts on buying it one day. Well, one day never came, because cancer came first and swallowed up our lives. *Her* life anyway. I was so angry when she was taken. She had less than a year with Lulu. Not anywhere near long enough for Lulu to remember her. But she sacrificed herself so that Lulu could have a rich, full life. I swore then and there that my neonatology practice would change."

"Ah..." Kirri tapped the side of her head. "I wondered what it was."

"What?"

"The thing that gave you the guts to do surgeries others don't."

A hit of gratitude exploded in his chest. He was glad she saw it that way. "Most folk call it insanity."

"Somebody has to be the pioneer." She put on a television announcer voice and intoned, *"He's the surgeon who will go where no man's gone before...* Or woman," she finished off brightly, then tucked her feet under her on the rocking chair seat.

Her expression was bereft of any judgement, just held interest.

"And if that courage is motivated by something emotional I think it clarifies the mission," she said.

Her choice of words piqued his interest. "What do you mean by 'mission'?"

"Well, you'll take calculated risks other people wouldn't dare to because you don't want anyone else to experience the sort of loss you have." She shook her head. "The way I see it, if a surgeon can do something about a problem—fix it—they should. You do that. Anyone who says otherwise is using common sense as a camouflage for their own fear."

Something told him she wasn't talking about his surgeries anymore, but her own research.

"Want to talk about it?" he asked.

She laughed at his echo of her words. "I suppose fair is fair—but you haven't really finished your story."

He took a drink of his tea, then nodded. Fair *was* fair. "The truth is, it feels like I've gone through a sea-change in only a matter of days."

"In what way?"

He traced a finger along her arm. "*You* arrived."

She gave a self-effacing laugh. "That's normally a signal for most men to run for the hills."

He locked her in a serious gaze. "I doubt that. If I were a guessing man, I'd imagine it was the other way round."

She feigned an air of indifference. "I'm just picky."

When their eyes met, a bit of her bravura wilted.

"Too picky, maybe."

Ty shook his head. There was no way he was going to let her take the fall for a step he didn't know how to take. "Don't do that. You deserve someone special, Kirri. Someone who can devote themselves to your happiness."

The idea that it could be someone else kicked him in the gut. Real hard. Did he have it in him to take this risk? To try, at least?

Kirri's cheeks had pinked up, but she was still shaking her head. "Everyone deserves full and complete love, but some of us take a lot longer to have room in their lives for it. And, of course…" she nodded at him "…some of us know just how high the bar really is and refuse to compromise."

It was a generous thing to say. Acknowledging his wife like that. Especially when he'd all but thrown a bucket of ice on an evening that had been a very obvious prelude to lovemaking. Apart from which, being with Kirri didn't feel like a compromise. It felt like a prize at the end of a long race. A prize that deserved to be cherished.

Ty lifted his mug in a toast. "You are wise beyond your years, young woman."

"Not so young, but I'll take the compliment."

She sniggered, but there was a hint of something he couldn't identify in her expression as she looked away.

Then, abruptly, she put down her mug and said, "I can't have children. That's my thing."

The hollowness and pain in her voice tore at his heart.

"I am *so* sorry." He reached out to take her hand but she shook her head. She didn't want comfort. Not for this.

Quickly, as if she'd made a deal with herself that she just had to blurt it out, she told him she had been born without a womb. MRKH syndrome. There had never been any chance she'd have a child. She'd found out when she was fifteen. The physical anomaly had colored her father's view of her. Put yet more distance between her and her mother. Doubled her drive to be recognized for her medical achievements as much as her brother was for his.

Her research was the only thing that kept her emotionally afloat, because it filled all those empty hours she would have loved to fill with a family of her own. And now her brother was insisting she cease and desist. Said it was destroying her rather than building her up.

She admitted there might be some truth to that. Her honesty was humbling. And the fact she could never have a child of her own and yet had devoted her life to helping others who could was little short of miraculous. Most people in her position would have walked away.

"I imagine loads of people have asked you this, but have you ever thought of—?"

"Adopting?" she finished for him. "No." She huffed out a sigh. "There was an ex… Andrew." She traced her finger along her mug. "I knew he wanted children and stupidly held off telling him I couldn't until it was too late."

"Too late for what?"

"Too late for my heart not to break when he dumped me for precisely that reason. Too late for the accusation that I'd never be a good mother anyway not to dig in and take hold."

Her voice sounded brittle with pain.

Ty's jaw tightened. "What an ass."

"Well…" She shrugged. "He wanted kids of his own. I couldn't give them to him. It may seem closed-minded of him not to have considered having children through another route—adoption, fostering—but ultimately I kept something from him that I shouldn't have. My deception came back and slapped me in the face."

"You shouldn't blame yourself for that."

She hung her head and sighed. "It's not like there's anyone else to blame. I became the person he said I was. Work-obsessed. Emotionally unavailable. Freaked out by kids."

"What? You were brilliant with Lulu and my sister's children."

Again she shrugged. It was still clearly a very raw subject.

She took a sip of her tea, then looked up at him. "I suppose the simple truth is I want what I can't have. That is how life works sometimes, isn't it? Wanting the one solitary thing you can't ever have and destroying everything else in your life in pursuit of the impossible."

Ty couldn't have put it better himself. He'd done his best with Lulu, but he knew that without his family propping him up she wouldn't be the well-rounded happy little girl she was today. His daughter was happy, but he knew she had the odd hit of envy for children who had mothers. A mother would love her in a way he never could because…well…because he was her father. No one could be both. No matter how hard they tried.

His brows tucked together as he took another long gulp of his hot drink. Did he want a wife? Someone to stand by his side and help him raise his daughter?

It was a question he had no capacity to answer in this exact moment, but he felt a closeness to Kirri he hadn't felt with anyone in years, and her honesty moved him to be forthright with her about the here and now.

"I truly did want to pick you up and carry you into this house."

She blinked her surprise. "You don't have to say that."

He took her hand in his, looked her in the eye and said, "I wanted to. Honestly. You are a beautiful, intelligent, sensitive, incredible woman. But when we got here and I saw the house..."

He wasn't sure he should go on, but if Kirri deserved anything it was honesty.

"I think the long and short of it is that the only woman I ever imagined carrying over that threshold was Gemma."

"And I'm not Gemma."

Saying the words felt like a knife in Kirri's heart.

She should have known better. Pulled back sooner. Never left the lab. Or Australia.

She pulled her hand out of Ty's and tucked her knees up under her chin, wrapping her arms around them so that she could look as small as she felt.

Just as she'd thought.

She wasn't good enough.

Not for Ty.

Not for her brother, who wanted to pen her into a surgical corner.

And she hadn't been enough for her father, who

had barely acknowledged the fact she'd graduated from med school and made something of herself.

She'd never been enough for the boyfriend she'd known wanted a family one day either.

"I think we'd better check on that taxicab."

"No. Kirri." Ty took her hand back in his and held it. "You've got it wrong. I *did* think that. It was a wobble. A big one. But I didn't waver for the reason you think."

She tugged her hand free again. "What other reason could possibly exist that would make you refuse to enter your house with me when we had driven here for the express purpose of doing— you know—*things*?"

Ty raked a hand through his hair, then seemed to make a decision. He pulled her into his arms, then tipped her chin up so that she was looking him straight in the eye.

"I freaked because I *could* picture carrying you into that house. I *could* picture ripping your clothes off. I freaked because when I kiss you my entire body is alight with fire and I don't ever want it to stop."

She shook her head. This was definitely not the explanation she'd been expecting. "That's a *good* thing, right?"

He tipped his head down to hers, his lips brushing against her mouth as he whispered, "I was scared. Scared right to my marrow. Because you make me feel like a brand-new man and that is one helluva change for a fellow to confront when he's falling for a woman who can't bowl for peanuts."

What little remained of her smile faltered. And then she kissed him. Hard. As if her life depended on it.

He kissed her back with a matching intensity, so perhaps it did. It seemed to at this moment, and that was all that mattered.

Before she could wrap her head around what was happening, she felt one of Ty's strong arms round her waist and the other shift under her buttocks. In one fluid move he lifted her up without a pause for breath. She wrapped her legs round his hips as he walked the pair of them through the front door.

It was a bold decision, and one she knew he wouldn't be taking lightly.

The pounding of their heartbeats synchronized as the door slammed shut behind them.

They made it as far as the stairwell. From there on out it was take no prisoners. Everything that had been pent up in them from that electric first moment of connection was unleashed in a torrent of feverish kisses, erotic caresses and the most delicate of touches.

Her T-shirt was gone in a trice. Then his shirt. Her boots. His jeans. Shoes, panties, boxers, bra—all gone. So that soon enough there was nothing between them but heat and desire.

Ty was everything she'd hoped for in a man and then some. Gentle. Passionate. Completely immersed in sharing with her the most vulnerable and beautiful moments a man and woman could share together.

"I can't get enough of you," he moaned as he dropped soft, seductive kisses along the length of her throat, his tongue flicking out for a swift lick when he hit that sweet dip between her collar bones.

She could feel the strength of his desire against her thighs as she pressed toward him and more than anything she wanted to share with him the ultimate intimacy. This wasn't sweet, slow lovemaking. This was carnal desire at its most divine apex.

She pushed him back so she could look into his face. "You're sure you want this?"

She saw everything in his eyes that she felt in her heart. Certainty.

"More than anything."

She parted her legs and groaned with pleasure as the tip of him, primed with desire, began to dip into the shallows of her essence.

Their groans of pleasure wove together above them as Ty pressed deeper, until in one swift, powerful move he was completely inside her.

Never before had she felt so complete. It was as if they had been made for one another.

His rhythm fine-tuned itself to hers. She pressed her hips up to meet him as stroke by fluid stroke they reached a climax as one.

He shifted the pair of them so that they lay on their sides, legs and arms tangled together as Kirri relished the sensations still rippling through her body.

They stayed like that for a while, their breaths steadying, the warmth of their bodies binding them together as tightly as the emotional connection she felt to Ty.

He knew her darkest secret and he'd still made love to her. He'd taken a step into the unknown for her. She'd never felt more treasured in her life than she did at this precise moment.

"What do you say we head upstairs?"

The way he said it left little doubt as to what he had in mind.

"Are you sure? Maybe I should get back to my place so that I'm not here when Lulu gets home."

He gave her a gentle smile and tucked a lock of stray hair behind her ear. "I think my mother and sisters knew what was happening before we did."

"What do you mean?"

"My sister sent a text. She'll be taking Lulu to Sunday school in the morning. We'll meet them at the house for lunch. Unless you have other plans?"

She gave him a playful poke on the chest. "You know jolly well my only plans were to try and break into the lab and hide out there for the rest of the weekend. You and your peach pies gave short shrift to that."

He leant in for a long slow kiss. "Tell me you didn't love it."

She wrapped her arms round him and pressed in close. She'd already shared so much with him. How could she tell him that spending the day with his family had been a dream come true? That tonight had been so much better than any icing on the very best of cakes? It was an entire pastry selection of unimaginable pleasure.

Were there complications?

A mountain's worth.

Things she had yet to tell him?

Ample.

Unknowns to confront, in the form of whether to tell his daughter, the fact that their lives were in different countries, the simple truth that she'd never be able to give him a big family like the one he was part of?

Thousands of them.

Were they worth ignoring in order to enjoy this incredibly perfect bubble of…was it love?

She looked into his eyes and saw nothing but

tenderness and compassion in them. She hoped he saw the same. It might not be love yet, but she already knew in her heart that the connection they shared would be something she would cherish forever.

"C'mon, you." He laced his fingers through hers and pulled her up. "How about I cancel that taxi of yours and we head on upstairs for some shut-eye?"

He dropped her a wink. The sort of wink that said they weren't anywhere *near* close to getting to sleep yet. But when they did sleep she knew she would be wrapped tight in his arms. And for that she was willing to let the world and her thousands of questions wait for another day.

CHAPTER NINE

Ty strode into the office with a lightness of step he hadn't felt in years.

It had been three weeks since he and Kirri had been together and about half an hour since he'd seen her last.

His family had embraced her as naturally as if she'd long since been one of their own.

His mother adored giving Kirri cooking lessons. She said her daughters already thought they knew better than her, so it was a genuine delight to have someone who actually listened to her for once.

This last weekend Kirri had insisted Lulu join them, because they had been learning how to make baking powder biscuits. A Southern essential, Marina had explained. Kirri and Lulu had finished the lesson covered in flour, but with huge smiles on their faces. The type of smiles that made him stuff his concerns about what he'd do in a few weeks' time to the back shelf. *Again.*

They'd agreed that circumstances dictated that whatever it was they were doing would only be an affair, but…*damn*…it felt a lot like falling in love. It was just so *natural*. Different from what he'd had with Gemma, but every bit as easy.

He was waiting for one of his sisters to invite him over to fix something, or for his father to take him out on a fishing trip. Both were family code for having "a talk". The type of talk that usually meant they thought whoever was on the receiving end was doing something stupid. But no one had said a word.

Last night Lulu had slept over with her cousins, so Ty had spent the night at Kirri's condo, enjoying the delights of the floor-to-ceiling view in between some rather athletic stints of lovemaking and a picnic of Mama Poppy's finest on the living room floor.

They hadn't told Lulu about the "special time" they shared together, seeing as Kirri would be going home in a few weeks, but he saw the way Lulu shone in Kirri's company. She loved showing off for her. Prancing about doing her dance moves from ballet class, singing her favorite songs, begging Kirri to watch the latest Disney film…

Put plainly, rather than resisting a woman coming into their lives, as Ty had feared, Lulu had taken to Kirri being a part of their family activities with arms wide open. As if she'd been waiting patiently all these years for this very specific flame-haired whirlwind to swirl in and shake up their lives.

Lulu clearly ached to have a woman in their lives. One who was there just for Ty and her. It worried him, because he knew there would come a time in the not too distant future when Kirri would leave, and Lulu wasn't the only one who would struggle to say goodbye.

Despite having agreed to keep their blossoming romance separate from their professional lives, the sly smiles and muffled giggles his staff regularly jiggled with when he wished them a good morning made it clear that the Piedmont grapevine was buzzing with the news that Dr. Sawyer had more than a hint of a spring in his step.

"Good morning, Stella."

As ever, the surgical nurse was waiting for him in the staff kitchen, with his coffee already poured and a list of the day's surgeries.

"Good morning to you, Dr. Sawyer." Her tone spoke volumes. She was the cat who'd got the cream. "I presume you had a lovely weekend?"

"Very." He accepted the coffee and took a long sip. "This is delicious."

"Same as ever, Dr. Sawyer."

He frowned at the mug and took another drink. Madness, he knew, but it felt like he was tasting coffee properly for the first time in years. All foods, really. He was seeing colors more brightly. Smelling the scents of spring with greater pleasure.

It was as if a filter had been lifted on his entire life. A gray, tasteless filter that had fallen into place when Gemma had got sick. It had robbed his life of beauty and, if he were being truly honest, of his natural vitality.

As a doctor, he knew cancer was rarely tactical. Taking out darkness with more darkness, it never took into account the kindness of the soul. The generosity of the person it would be robbing loved ones of. The parent the child would never know…

His wife's words tugged at his heart in a way they never had before.

"You'll know, sweetheart. It may take a while, but you'll know. And for heaven's sake do something about it."

"You look different."

Stella tipped her head forward so that she was looking at him over the rims of her glasses. It was the type of sage look a television psychologist might give to someone who had finally turned a corner.

He didn't bother asking different to what. He knew. He looked as if he'd rejoined the land of the living.

"You going to do something about it?" she asked.

He smiled at her but didn't answer.

His gut churned at the thought of taking Kirri to the airport. He of all people knew how precious time was and how critical it was to make the most of it. He of all people knew the physical, soul-sucking pain of saying goodbye forever.

This time he didn't have to.

If he didn't say something, *do* something, he knew he'd spend the rest of his life wondering if he had let the best thing that had happened to him in the last five years walk right out of his life.

He wanted her to stay as much as he wanted to draw breath. But asking her to do so would be selfish. It would be a huge sacrifice. One he didn't know he could ask her to make. Apart from the complications of the specialized visa she'd needed for the trip, they'd already allocated the clinic's research funding and the all important 3D printer for the next three years. For the foreseeable future, at least, Kirri wouldn't be able to use their labs. Would working on the surgical ward and loving him and Lulu be enough?

He honestly didn't know. But he'd never find out if he didn't ask, and he sure as hell was going to try.

As if she'd followed his entire train of thought, Stella gave him one of her wise owl smiles.

"Don't think I'm pushing, but if I were in your shoes I know what I'd do."

She popped on a bright smile.

"Right!" Stella turned toward the door. "Are you going to stand there all day, sipping that cup of coffee like it's honey and nectar, or are you going to get into that scrub room and start saving some babies' lives?"

He smiled and laughed, clapped an arm round Stella's shoulders as they headed toward the surgical unit. "Let's do it. Let's go save some lives."

Kirri pushed back from her microscope and sighed. She was well and truly struggling. As advanced as this 3D cell-structure model was, there were still miles to go before she could get the culture model to mimic the uterus's true cellular properties.

A warm, cuddly sensation swirled through her as she reminded herself that Ty had said not to worry about epic breakthroughs. She wasn't here to score the goals. She was here to be a player in the game.

Trouble was, she still wanted to be the *best* player. It was part of her genetic fabric to push on, no matter how hard the battle.

She tipped her head into her hands and tried to get the facts straight. There were literally so many microscopic factors her mind kept fuzzing with the details.

"Anything I can help with?" asked Gloria, the researcher who was sitting next to her.

"Not unless you can figure out how to create a hydrogel membrane that perfectly mimics the placenta."

Gloria whistled, then shook her head. "That's well out of my sphere of knowledge, girlfriend. You need to be over in Vienna for that sort of action."

"Vienna?"

"Yeah…"

She tugged out the shoulder bag stashed under her desk and rifled through it until she unearthed a magazine that specialized in reporting on medical innovations. She turned it around and tapped the cover story.

"I thought you would've been all over this and packing your bags."

Kirri frowned at the magazine cover.

Scientists make significant breakthrough with artificial placenta model

Gloria handed her the magazine. "If I were you I'd be on the phone to these guys today. How's your German?"

Schlecht, Kirri thought darkly.

Seeing the article made her feel like she'd been ripped in two.

She'd been trying to think of a way to ask Ty about extending her stay here in Atlanta, but what they were doing in Vienna…it was exactly what she'd been looking for professionally for just about forever.

When Gloria turned back to her Petri dishes Kirri began to rapidly scan the article, one word blurring into the next as she read about the hi-tech bio-med team who had made the breakthrough. They were miles ahead of her. Well, a good meter anyway. This sort of research progressed painful millimeter by millimeter, and what they'd achieved was little short of a miracle.

If she'd been feeling more positive she would be congratulating herself on getting as far as she had on her own. They had an entire team and proper funding. She had been pouring her own salary into buying all the necessary equipment herself. It was why coming here to Atlanta had been a godsend. Her brother paid her handsomely, but there was no chance she'd ever be able to buy her own 3D printer.

Words kept popping out at her. *Laser beams. Hydrogel. Biocompatibility.*

When she got to the end of the article she saw that the reason they'd begun their experiment was to explore critical research issues regarding the nutrient exchange between mother and child. Her endgame went much further. The baby grow bag.

Seeing this breakthrough lauded with such acclaim made one thing crystal-clear. If she wanted to make the sorts of strides she believed were possible she needed to go to Vienna.

Her brother's wrath she could deal with.

But the look in Ty's eyes when she told him she'd be tearing this fragile thing they were building in two… The thought churned in her like bile.

She put the article down, her fingers shaking so hard she had to press them to the lab table. Who knew how much truth there was in it? Articles like this surfaced all the time.

Not like this one, they didn't.

She forced herself to look at her work from a different angle. Knowing new things sometimes brought fresh perspective.

An hour later she'd hit a wall.

It was no good. The Austrian team's development had hit her right where it hurt. In the ego. If she'd had their resources, and a whole team dedicated to this one solitary project, she'd be the one on the magazine cover.

If she went to Vienna she could be.

Her heart constricted so hard and fast she pushed away from her desk and left the lab. She needed thinking time.

Without even remembering how she'd got

there, she found herself on the surgical floor, looking for the tall, dark-haired brainiac who set her world alight in the opposite way her research did. Balance, happiness, fun…

He has a child.

A child she was falling in love with every bit as much as she was falling for Ty.

It was such unfamiliar territory…and yet she was finally beginning to see how loving a child didn't have to be the complicated web of emotions she'd always made it out to be.

Kirri had kept all children at arm's length because she'd never thought she could love one properly. Ty had clearly seen something in her that believed otherwise and it had given her confidence. Perhaps it was simpler than that. Maybe she and Lulu just clicked. The same way she and Ty had on that first rain-soaked morning.

From the most barren earth comes little grass shoots…

Tingles of anticipation shot through her when she heard his voice around the corner. Her fingers flexed in anticipation of joining him. It hit her that she hadn't felt this fired up about being in the operating theater since… Well, since she'd started researching the baby grow bag.

Boring old facts slammed into her. Surgery was fun right now because she was—honesty check—she was completely giddy with romance.

That buzzy, elated feeling wouldn't last forever. If it became love it might, but the way things were on a professional front definitely wouldn't stay the same.

The research lab here was chock-a-block for the next few years and the queue after that was crazy long. She could do surgery fulltime, but would it be enough? More to the point, would she have the strength to step away from the way she defined herself—her work—to have a proper life with Lulu and Ty? Was she brave enough? Humble enough to accept that it wouldn't all be plain sailing? Hopeful enough to know that the rewards would be far better than being on the cover of any magazine? That ignoring Vienna would be worth it even if she might never make her father proud?

She ducked her head into the scrub room and, as she'd hoped, found Ty there, going through the familiar motions. It was almost meditative, watching him. The care he took. Nails, hands, forearms… All scrubbed in preparation for being gowned and masked in order to change a tiny person's life.

She knocked on the doorframe to get his attention. When he turned and saw her that gorgeous smile of his warmed her from the inside out. Saying goodbye to this man was going to be like ripping an organ out of her gut. A vital life-force she'd never known she needed.

"Need an extra pair of hands?"

His eyes sparked as he nodded. "You should definitely scrub in on this one. Keyhole spine repair for a baby with spina bifida."

Adrenaline shot through her. This was cutting-edge stuff. "Amazing! I'd love to be a part of that. Why didn't you tell me?"

"It's Mark's surgery, really. I'm scrubbing in as an extra pair of hands." He gave her a cheeky grin. "I did actually come up to the lab to tell you about it an hour ago, but you looked so serious I thought I'd better leave you to it."

"*Moi?* Serious?"

She jested to cover her nerves. He'd seen her frowning in the wake of reading about the Vienna discovery. Thank goodness he couldn't read minds.

"Deadly," he said, his eyes connecting with hers. They narrowed. "Is everything all right with you? You seem a bit distracted."

Just trying to figure out whether to follow my head to Vienna or my heart to Atlanta.

"Kirri?"

Nuts. He knew something was up. He was getting good at reading her body language. Too good.

Would it be so bad to have someone know

you that well? Someone to help you weather the storms?

Her shoulders shifted up to her ears, then dropped heavily. "I am."

He glanced at the OR, where the staff were beginning to enter from the other scrub room. "I've got to get in there, darlin'. You are more than welcome to join us. Whatever it is—I have no doubt everything'll work out for the best."

With every fiber in her being she wanted to believe him. But she'd once believed in Santa Claus.

Was whatever it was they were sharing just a fiction, brought about by her short-term contract, or was this like the spirit of Christmas, which overrode every child's discovery that Santa wasn't real? Eternal, enduring, magic.

"Can you grab that pile of blankets, please, Kirri?"

Henry pointed at the back of the family's SUV as he and Ty hauled a cool box over to where the family was setting up a picnic.

"Absolutely."

Her gaze caught and snagged on Ty. Her man. Her temporary man, anyway. He was looking tanned and gorgeous and, most of all, completely and utterly relaxed. A far cry from the uptight, speed-walking hunk of sexy Ice King she'd met on that first day. The one whose chink had appeared in the form of an umbrella and glints of gold in his eyes.

Tingles of delight at the memory skittered through her, and then again as she mentally replayed the soft kiss they'd stolen today, before the children had all piled out of their grandparents' house and into the cars.

Part of her had felt like the naughty teenager she'd never had a chance to be. *Thanks, Dad.* The other part of her had felt utterly content in a way she'd never imagined possible.

Nothing had ever felt so natural to her as being part of Ty and Lulu's lives. They were busy. Work, Lulu's numerous activities and plain old life got in the way of loads of "Ty and Kirri" time. But when they had some it was pure gold dust. In all honesty, it was *all* gold dust. One huge hunk of glowing golden nugget.

"Here, let me help you honey."

Ty's sister Tammy bustled in beside her and tugged out the mammoth pile of picnic rugs and homemade quilts that seemed far too beautiful to spread on a grassy field in the park—but that was exactly what they were doing.

"Now that you're part of the posse that pile just keeps getting bigger and bigger."

Instead of taking the comment as a slight, as she might have a few weeks ago—hypersensitivity being one of her superpowers—Kirri felt well and truly welcomed by it. She was part of a "posse"!

Up until now she'd been used to putting herself to the side at group activities—waiting for the natural pairings to take place and then sticking herself on an edge ready for a quick escape. Not here. And definitely not with the Sawyers running the show. They were all for one and one for all. It felt incredibly enriching to be a part of such a happy family.

She squeezed her eyes against the twist of emotion that inevitably followed any sort of reminder that her time here came with a ticking clock.

"You all right, hon?"

Tammy shifted the stack of quilts to her hip and caught her in a little half-hug.

"Yeah, of course. I just…" She watched as a tumble of cousins and in-laws grabbed picnic baskets, the family dogs and each other, then made their way to the site that Winny had pegged out for them, holding her newborn.

"I just wish my brother could see this. See me." Lucius would think she'd gone clinically insane.

Tammy's brow furrowed. "Why? You have open-air movies in Sydney, don't you?"

"Yes, but—" She'd never been. She doubted Lucius had.

The point was, the Sawyers were doing it as a *family*. And she felt part of that family. Rather than feeling less valued than any of them, because she couldn't have children, she felt valued simply for being *her*. Not that they knew her secret—Ty had honored her request to keep that private—but for the first time in her life she didn't mind if people knew. These people, anyway.

With crystal-clear clarity Kirri knew without a shadow of a doubt that her whole "don't date men with children" rule had been a form of denial. She'd been denying herself a love she'd thought she wasn't worthy of when in actual fact it was a love she *could* give. A love she craved like air.

She'd spent all these years being terrified of failing. Sticking to her workaholic routine as if it were the thing keeping her alive, and not the hopes and dreams she'd stuffed into a cupboard all those years ago when her ex had made her feel valueless.

"Why don't you call him? Your brother?" Tammy nodded at the pocket she knew Kirri kept her phone in. "Do one of those video calls. Show him what a good time you're having. We'll all cheer and wave!"

"Oh…it's about five in the morning at home. Better not."

Five in the morning but her brother would be up, having his first cup of coffee and preparing for another long day at Harborside. She definitely wasn't the only workaholic in the family.

Besides, calling him up when she was having such a brilliant time outside the lab would be like salt in the wound. Proof, if he needed any, that she wasn't prioritizing Harborside above all else. Not to mention the fact he'd feel a thousand shades of awkward with all the kissing and the hugging and the general being in and out of each other's business that Ty's family enjoyed so much. Little wonder, since the pair of them had virtually been raised to be lone wolves…

But…oh, it was lovely here. Her heart felt as though it was healing from wounds she'd never even known she'd endured.

Her father would balk at most of the activities that seemed to bring the Sawyers so much joy. Goofing around with the sprinkler in the back garden. Cheering on the grandchildren at their Little League games as if they were watching the World Series. And, of course, things like tonight. Bundling everyone—seventeen of them in total—into a virtual motorcade's worth of cars and heading down to Atlantic Station's recently renovated Central Park to watch an open-air movie and eat—a mountain of barbecue, of course.

It was a vivid reminder that perhaps there was a bit more to life than Petri dishes and—she could hardly believe she was even *thinking* this—3D printers.

Which made knowing that her fantasy lab was sitting in Vienna, glowing away like a whole different type of magical kingdom, that much harder. The question was, was it an illusion or the type of magical kingdom where dreams really did come true?

Depends upon what the dream is, you goose. Depends upon what the dream is.

As the cartoon before the main film flickered to life they finally decanted everything from the cars, and the children were soon parked in front of huge banana leaf trays of chicken wings and barbecued ribs.

Her phone rang.

Lucius.

She signaled to Tammy that she'd be back in a moment and took the call. "Hey, Luce. What's up?"

"*Someone* sounds like they're not in a lab preparing to change the world."

The words didn't come laced with venom, but they definitely hit their mark.

She had been slacking—if working regular office hours could officially be called slacking.

A well of frustration balled in her belly. Why didn't she seem to be able to get the balance right?

Because there had been no balance in her old life.

Guilt poured in as she shot a glance toward the

downtown area, where her research was sitting all by itself in a darkened lab. It wouldn't exactly be crying itself to sleep at night, but she wasn't here to have jollies out in the park with a family she was going to have to say goodbye to. With a man who'd made her see life from an entirely new angle. She was here to work.

But they were so persuasive!

"The fresh air will do you good!"

"You *must* see a movie in the park—there is the *best* popcorn."

"You've never seen *Singing in the Rain*?"

"Too late! I've booked you a ticket."

That last had been from Ty. He'd run his fingers along her arm as he told her, knowing his touch was all the persuasion she needed.

Lucius didn't wait for a response. "Have you booked your flight yet?"

Her eyes hooked with Ty's across the picnic ground and he waved her over. She signaled that she'd be a minute. He smiled and dropped her a slow wink that sent ripples of approbation through her. Twenty meters away and the man could still give her butterflies. Hell, they didn't even have to be in the same *room* and he gave her butterflies.

Would it be the same if she was on a different continent?

"Kirri?"

"There's one with seats a fortnight from today."

It was a lie. She had booked an open return and hadn't yet checked. And there was also Vienna to consider.

"Right, then. Book it."

She definitely would, but... *Oh, God.* Suddenly the thought of going back to her old life felt like depriving this new self she was discovering of oxygen. It wasn't Lucius's fault. Not at all. And the lure to stay was so much stronger than the amazing sex she was having...although that helped. The truth lay with one incredible man—and his daughter, if she was being completely honest—whom she was falling madly in love with.

Could true love happen that fast? In the blink of an eye?

It certainly felt like it.

But was it a love that could endure distance? Long hours at the lab? A dedication to something outside the family unit?

Living her life without the pressure of having to deliver results in order to be valued had been a revelation. And it was Ty who had made her see that. He had made it clear to her time and again that her research was one hundred percent about getting a fresh perspective. Not about results. He'd even teased her the other night, as he'd dropped some rather scrumptious kisses onto her belly, that if she did come up with a breakthrough he'd have to fire her.

He'd been joking, of course, but the freedom to think and explore, to let her imagination run wild with her project, was all thanks to the amazing man she was staring at right now.

He was hoisting Lulu up onto his back for a quick piggyback ride to the popcorn stall. Her heart ached to be with them. She wanted it all. The love, the work, the emotional rewards of living a rich and colorful tapestry of a life.

"Kirri? Is there a time delay or something on this line?" Lucius was getting impatient now.

"No—sorry. I'm here."

In Atlanta. And so is my heart.

"Good. Book your flight."

"I will." She would.

"And the sooner the better. The locums you hired are chomping at the bit, wondering whether they need to stay or go. And they're not the only ones who are wondering."

"Oh, well…"

She wanted to tell him to book them forever. Hire the best. To say, *You don't need me there. You never did. You were only doing what a big brother does. Care and protect. But I don't need you to look after me anymore, big brother. I need to spread my wings. See what I can do under my own steam.*

"I need a proper answer by the end of the week, Kirri."

Three more days.

She pictured herself back at the beautiful cutting-edge clinic her brother helmed and began to feel the oxygen leaving her lungs. Then she did the same with the lab in Vienna.

She could hardly breathe.

"You'll have your answer," she managed, though she already knew in her heart what she wanted.

Was she brave enough to ask for it?

"Fine." Lucius, as per usual, hung up the phone before she could tell him what she really felt.

I love you. I miss you. I wish we were closer.

And she wasn't just talking about geography. She meant close like Ty was with his sisters. But merely *thinking* of telling Lucius she loved him felt scary. Rejection was such an inbuilt factor in their family life, the idea of admitting she loved him set her stomach churning.

He's had your back all these years. Why would he stop now?

He'd put up with a lot more than any other boss would. And she owed him. She owed him her full commitment back in Sydney at the Harborside Fertility and Women's Neonatal Center.

Ty and Lulu appeared by her side as she pocketed her phone.

Ty gave her a quick squeeze, then slipped his hand into hers as Lulu took her other hand, her arm wrapped round a huge tub of popcorn.

"Everything okay, Kirri? The movie's starting."

Ty's brow furrowed as he tried to read her mood.

"Fine. Just a work call."

He gave her a sharp look. He knew work calls at this time of night only meant one thing. A work call from home.

"Urgent?"

"No," she managed to choke out. "Just a bit of forward-planning."

A flash of dismay lit and then darkened Ty's eyes. He was clever. He knew it had been Lucius and that they'd been talking about her return to Sydney.

"C'mon, Kirri." Lulu tugged at her hand. "I want to sit on your lap when we watch the movie."

Kirri looked down into the little girl's dark eyes—a perfect reflection of her father's—and saw pure, unbridled expectation in them.

Leaving Ty would be one thing, and just thinking about it unleashed a level of pain she didn't know if she could handle. Leaving Lulu would be a whole new brand of heartache. Kirri didn't know if she had it in her to do it.

In just a handful of weeks this chirpy little

squirt of a girl had wormed her way into her heart in a way no child ever had. The mere idea of bringing tears to Lulu's eyes filled her with dread. And Kirri knew the pain she felt in her chest only hinted at the true responsibility that came with loving a child.

Did she have what it took to offer the type of commitment to Ty and Lulu they deserved?

Her eyes flitted back to the Medical Innovations Center skyscraper.

Did it have to be a choice?

"If you want to make a name for yourself you have to make choices. Success requires sacrifice."

Her father's voice sent a chilling numbness through her. A personal life or a professional legacy. That's what it seemed to boil down to. She'd dedicated years of her life to her research. Could she give it up for something that didn't come with a guarantee?

Nothing comes with a guarantee, you dill. Not science, not medicine, not love.

She felt the little girl's fingers in her right hand and the strong, caring man's hand in her left.

The time had come to make a decision.

CHAPTER TEN

Ty PULLED KIRRI in close to him and whispered, "We have ten more floors, if you're game…"

Kirri snuggled up close to him and spoke in a low husky voice she'd not heard come out of her throat before. "Game for what, exactly?"

Ty tipped his lips down to meet hers and showed her.

By the time the lift doors opened on the Piedmont Women and Baby Pavilion Kirri knew her mouth looked as though she'd used a glossy plumper on her lips. Kissing the man of your dreams had a way of doing that to a girl.

"See you later for that gastroschisis?"

Kirri nodded. "Absolutely."

They waved goodbye and Kirri jogged up the stairwell to the research lab. In all honesty she was keen to do any and all the surgeries Ty invited her to. She was loving it in the surgical ward—and not just because Ty was there. For the first time in ages she didn't feel surgery was something she *had* to do before she was allowed to do what she *wanted* to do.

A few hours into the day the phone rang. It was for Kirri.

When she finished the call her insides were vibrating with conflicting emotions.

"You all right, sugar?" Gloria asked, just as Ty entered the lab.

Her eyes shot to Ty's.

"Everything okay?" he asked.

Kirri nodded dumbly.

Ty was by her side in an instant. "Kirri. Talk to me. Is everything all right?"

"Yes. I…um… That was the research team in Vienna."

"The one you were telling me about?"

She nodded. She'd showed him the article the night before. He'd nodded. Said it looked interesting. Then he'd put it aside as easily as if she'd shown him an article on peach blossom. Interesting, but no earthquakes.

"They want me to go and work with them in Vienna."

Gloria clapped her hands. "I *knew* it was worth it."

Kirri's eyes snapped to hers. "What do you mean?"

"I might've accidentally on purpose forwarded

them your résumé. You can thank me later in the form of a strawberry daiquiri. Large."

Gloria clapped again and turned around to her microscope, humming a happy little tune.

"Are you going to take up the offer?" Ty's voice was neutral but his eyes had gone a shade of dark she'd never seen before.

"I told them I need to think about it."

She saw the impact of her words in an instant. Ty was trying to look supportive, but she could see that the last thing he'd thought she'd do was jump on a plane to Vienna. In all honesty she'd thought the same thing, but... It was a chance of a lifetime.

She began to babble on about everything they did. The lab. The number of scientists involved in the project. The biochemists. And the *funding*. Oh, man, the funding was out of this world. No wonder they'd made such leaps. And if she put her research with their research, who knew what would happen?

Too late she realized she might have let her enthusiasm for the Vienna team boil over. "Maybe we could talk about it after work?"

He gave her a curt nod. "I promised Lulu homemade pizza and a movie. Up for that?"

She nodded, unable to say what she really wanted. *Forever and always...*

It was the chance of a lifetime.

But so was what she had with Ty.

She didn't want to choose, but she knew deep in her heart that she had to. A life of intellectual plaudits and groundbreaking medical innovation was what she'd always dreamed of.

She'd also always dreamed of being loved.

Ty was gone before she had a chance to communicate to him what she hoped he already knew. That this was difficult. That she would've already been on the way to the airport if she hadn't met him. But she had. And as such she had a decision to make.

It had been a night filled with the unspoken, and Ty was feeling increasingly agitated.

He didn't want to stop Kirri from following her heart. Couldn't. His entire ethos at the clinic was to inspire and then watch as his staff moved on and grew. But he'd never fallen in love with a person he was meant to set free before.

It tore his heart in two to have to let her go, but hobbling her passion for research was the last thing he was going to do. No relationship could survive that sort of blow.

"C'mon, Kirri!" Lulu ran up the stairs. "It's book at bedtime!"

Ty noted Kirri's hesitation as he headed up the stairs in his daughter's wake. "You're welcome to join us," he told her.

Kirri's brow crinkled. He could almost see the wheels whirling behind her dark blue eyes.

"I don't want to get in the way of any rituals."

He almost laughed. She'd already broken through *that* barrier the day she'd come to Chuck's Charcoal Heaven with them. Bowling. Movie nights. Baseball games. Tonight had been just a simple meal at home and a movie on TV. Even though the tension of her decision had been buzzing between them, the house had felt more like a home than it ever had.

He didn't want that feeling to vanish. He didn't want *her* to vanish. But he would not be held responsible for crushing her dreams.

Lulu appeared at the top of the stairs, brandishing a book. "Kirri! Can you read me my story tonight?"

Kirri's eyes sought Ty's as if seeking permission.

"Maybe Kirri's a bit tired, darlin'."

He hoped not. He needed to talk to her. As they'd left work she'd told him that not only did the center in Vienna want an answer by tomorrow, so did Lucius. And then she'd turned on the radio.

"I want Kirri to read it," Lulu insisted. "She does the kangaroo voice better."

A smile lit up Kirri's face and she put on a

goofy voice and bounced up the stairs. "That's because kangaroos are Australian."

"Just like you!"

"That's right!" She reached the top landing. "Just like me."

Her eyes caught with Ty's and in that instant he knew Kirri was in the exact same boat as he was. Desperately trying to make the very best decisions about her future. He saw affection and warmth and maybe even love in those eyes, but there was also that critical hint of reservation.

His heart bashed against his ribcage. He didn't want to let her go. He was a better man when he was with her. A better doctor. A better father. That part had taken some getting used to, but she was amazing with Lulu. Particularly considering how difficult he knew it was for her to be with children.

He went to the bedroom door and watched as Lulu snuggled up to Kirri, who was stretched out alongside her on the butterfly quilt his mother had made for her a couple of years back. She looked perfectly relaxed and Lulu's entire demeanor oozed contentment.

Lulu's index finger was resting atop Kirri's as she traced along the words she was reading, hopping up occasionally when the text shifted from dialogue to *"Boing! Boing! Boing!"*

It was a heartwarming moment he'd never

thought he'd experience without feeling the searing pain of grief and loss. It was, of course, the kind of moment he thought he'd be sharing with Gemma. And now he would no longer be sharing them with Kirri.

As painful as it was, he knew it was the right decision. He would encourage her to go.

Kirri glanced up and saw Ty in the doorway. She'd been so engrossed in reading the story she hadn't noticed anything other than Lulu's little fingers resting on her own, and now the weight of her young body as she drifted off to sleep, using Kirri as a pillow.

"Everything all right?" he asked.

Perfect, she mouthed, and then said aloud, "Catch up with you downstairs in a minute?"

Ty nodded with a smile. A knowing smile. He'd had six years of moments like this. This was her first—and, boy, was it out of this world?

She glanced at the bedside table and saw a small framed picture of a woman holding a baby in her arms. Gemma and Lulu, she presumed. Tears stung at the back of her throat as she imagined how heartbreaking it must have been for Gemma to know she'd never have a moment like this. Reading her daughter a story. Having her fall asleep in her arms. Curling into her as if she were the safest person in the world to love.

Behind the picture she saw another photo that had been taped to the wall. It was Ty, Kirri and Lulu, each brandishing a bowling ball on that very first night they'd been out for barbecue. They were all beaming. Especially Lulu, who wasn't looking at the camera. She was looking at Kirri.

She inhaled a bit more of the sweet scent of Lulu's hair as she eased her down into a nest of pillows surrounded by a rainbow of cuddly toys. Not quite ready to leave, she knelt by the bed and stroked her silky dark hair, memorizing the freckles that ran across her little button nose, her cherubic smile and the dimple on her left cheek.

Moments like this felt like they were virtually impossible to give up. No wonder single dads were protective of their little ones. Who'd want to shoulder the burden of breaking their children's hearts by introducing someone into their lives and only to take them away? Ty had taken quite a risk, letting her into their lives like this. It showed a level of courage she wasn't sure *she* possessed.

She ran her fingers through Lulu's hair and knew in that moment that she could definitely love a child who wasn't her own. She could love Lulu. Probably already did. Love was love. Kirri would never have any idea what it would be like to love a child of her own, so why compare the two? Love came in all different forms, didn't it?

The love of an idea. A dream. Brotherly love. The love you had for a parent, no matter how unreciprocated or conditional it was.

She thought of the job in Vienna. Was it the final hurdle she must leap to grasp her father's attention? Or would there be another and another, until in the end she would realize it had all been for nothing? Her father—and her mother, come to think of it—truly weren't capable of that type of love. Selfless, generous, unconditional love.

Lulu nestled into her hand, making sweet little-girl sleepy noises as she did so.

Kirri's heart felt as though it were being torn in two.

Maybe it was time to give up the childhood dream of winning her father's approval. Ty's family had accepted Kirri into their lives as easily as they would have welcomed one of their own. Couldn't that be enough?

The only thing she wasn't a thousand percent sure of was…

"Hey, darlin'…"

Ty appeared again in the doorframe. His eyes dropped from hers to his daughter's cheek, nestled in Kirri's hand. His expression was more serious than she'd ever seen it.

"Do you mind if we have a little chat before you go?"

Uh-oh. She'd overstepped.

This was precisely why she'd never let her feelings run away with her before—because now that she'd had a taste of what her dream life could be like bearing the loss of it might be more than she could handle. No amount of research would ever make up for this. For Ty. For Lulu. For the life she now knew she desperately wanted to live.

She followed behind him, her heart in her throat, waiting to hear the words she'd feared hearing all along: *I'm afraid this isn't going to work.*

Ty thought he'd experienced the definition of a hammering heart before now—but, no. He had not. If his heart didn't watch it, it would punch straight through his ribcage and out onto the back porch.

"Everything okay?" Kirri asked as she sat down on the porch swing.

She looked as nervous as he felt.

He sat down on the swing beside her. "Fine. No. That's not entirely true." He stroked his fingers along her cheek. "I've never been better. Up until about two o'clock this afternoon, that is. Never been better." He heard the emotion in his own voice and forced himself to carry on. "And I think you know the reason why."

"Go on."

Kirri's features had softened with a wash of

emotions that made saying what he had to a thousand times harder.

"I think you should go to Vienna." He held up a hand when she opened her mouth. "As you know, we can't offer you ongoing research here. Not the type they can. All I can offer is a post on the surgical ward, which I know isn't where your heart is, so…"

Damn this was hard.

"If you really want to make those strides forward, it seems like Vienna's the best place for you."

His voice sounded like a stranger's. The voice of a man he'd never want to meet.

"Fair enough."

Kirri's voice was barely audible. And it contained traces of a bitterness he hadn't expected to hear.

"It's what you want, isn't it?"

"Of course." She gave a strangled sort of laugh. "I can hardly believe I'm not on a plane right now. I was just…you know…fulfilling the criteria of our contract."

Had he messed up? Got the wrong end of the stick? She'd just seemed so energized when the job offer came through. Jubilant, even.

"Look…" He took both her hands in his. They lay limply in his palms. "We will give you the highest of recommendations, of course. Not that you need them, seeing as you already have the job. I just want you to know that what we've shared outside of the office these past few weeks—"

Something flickered across her eyes that he couldn't pin down. Before he could put a name to it she blinked and replaced her shocked expression with a bright smile.

"Good!" She pulled her hands out of his, rubbed them on her thighs, then gave them a clap together. "Happy to know I have your professional support."

Ty began to flounder. Had he read her enthusiasm the wrong way? Surely this was what she wanted?

"If it was surgery you were after I'd be offering you a contract in a minute, but Piedmont isn't the best place for you—"

She waved her hands for him to stop. "Please. I get it. You're being very generous." She popped on a very bad German accent. "I love *schnitzel und kuchen*. Vienna vill be amazink!"

She looked anything but happy.

"Kirri, please don't think I'm saying this because I don't believe in you. It's not that at all. You know as well as I do that Piedmont isn't the right place for the type of leaps you're hoping to make. Vienna is—Japan is."

Kirri abruptly stood up. "Yes, well... Lucky

for me I like sushi, too." She pulled out her phone and opened the app for a taxi.

A few deeply uncomfortable minutes later it arrived, and without so much as a backward look she disappeared into the night.

Walking up the stairs toward his bedroom, he felt like he was hauling boulders of grief. He'd just said goodbye to the woman he loved. Why did doing the right thing have to come at such a cost?

Lulu appeared in the doorway. "Papa? Has Kirri gone for the night?"

Worse. She'd very likely gone for good.

"I'm afraid so, little one."

Lulu's lower lip quivered. "Has she gone forever?"

Ty looked blindly out toward the street and silently pulled his daughter into his arms, so she wouldn't see the anguish in his face. Something core-deep told him it *was* forever. And that it was all his fault. He'd just hammered a nail into a coffin he'd built himself.

"You were right. I was wrong!" Kirri shouted at her phone as she haphazardly threw a blouse into her suitcase.

There was no point in packing things nicely because she never wanted to look beautiful for anyone ever again. Not after this fiasco.

How could she have thought Ty loved her?

I think you should go.

The words echoed in a loop in her head. If only there was a way to turn it off.

He wanted her to go.

This felt about a million times worse than when her ex had dumped her all those years ago. Worse because now she knew *exactly* what she was missing. And Lulu! How could he have let her cuddle Lulu like that when he knew he was going to give her the brush-off?

Pure, unadulterated heartbreak. That was what she was feeling.

The only way he could have been more blunt would have been for him to say, *It's all been a mistake. So sorry. My bad! Here's your ticket out of town—now go.*

"G'day, Kirri." Her brother's voice was as dry as ever. "I see someone woke up on the wrong side of the bed."

"Oh, stuff you and your niceties." Kirri wasn't in the mood for witty banter. In fairness, she wasn't in the mood for anything except for crying. Weeping or raging. Those were her two options. So she'd chosen the latter and she was taking it out on her big brother. He was stoic. He could take it.

She threw in a pair of heels she never should

have packed. Fancy nights out on the town. What had she been *thinking*?

"What am I right about?"

"Coming to Piedmont for research."

"Why? I thought I was going to have drag you out of there kicking and screaming."

He was. Right up until the minute she'd figured out Ty didn't love her as much as she loved him.

"It was a set-up," she snapped.

It wasn't, but saying as much made her feel better.

"What? The thing in Piedmont?"

"*Yes*, the thing at Piedmont! What else would we be talking about?"

"Well…"

Lucius's deep voice came across the line as clearly as if he was sitting next to her.

"I was thinking it might be about the reference request I just received from a certain biochemistry clinic in Vienna."

"Oh." She flopped down on the side of the bed. "That."

"Looks like the opportunity of a lifetime."

"It is."

A sob caught in her throat. It was the perfect job offer for an over-emotional, highly charged, heartbroken Australian doctor intent on filling the baby void and now the love void with all-consuming research.

She scooped up a pair of socks from the floor and threw them into her suitcase.

"Kirri, back up. Will you please explain to me, as if I am simpleton, what the hell is going on? I thought you were getting on blue blazes there."

Her heart was breaking. That was what was going on.

"I am. Well, on the surgical floor. Not so much on the research floor, which is why Ty thinks I should go."

He also didn't love her. If he did, he'd hardly be pushing her out the door, would he?

More tears cascaded down her cheeks. She didn't even know why she'd called Lucius. It wasn't like he was going to offer her any advice beyond telling her to come back and get to work. No. This was it. Her future was mapped out. She was going to become a *lederhosen*-wearing science nerd who ate cake for supper. And there'd be a cat. She'd need at least one prescient being in her life to care if she lived or died.

Lucius didn't say anything. Her insides churned with frustration. If she was going to feel awful about this one thing then she wanted to feel awful about everything in her life. Get it all over with.

"Did he say that he thought your research was useless?" Lucius asked.

No. He hadn't.

"He said he thought I should follow my passion elsewhere because this wasn't the place to pursue it."

A thick silence hummed between them.

"Oh, go on! Say it. I know what you're thinking!" she said.

"I don't think you do."

"Well, I do. You're thinking, *Good. Someone else has finally had the guts to tell my sister to stop her research. It's utterly pointless, so she might as well pick up her scalpel and get back to the operating theater, because it's the only thing she's any good for.*"

"I think you might be missing a few critical points here, Kirri."

She glared at the phone. Typical Lucius. Couldn't he simply listen to her rage and then say *There, there, everything's going to be all right*, like Ty would? Well, like Ty would have if she hadn't stormed off and left him to get on with the rest of his life without her.

She sighed and said a conciliatory, "Like what?"

"Well, like the compliments he's given you, for one."

"What compliments? He said he invited me here never expecting me to have a breakthrough."

"Really?"

"Yeah. Really. He expected absolutely nothing of me. Just like Dad."

"Don't compare other people to Dad."

"Why not?"

Lucius's tone darkened. "He's in a league of his own." He took a sharp inhalation, then continued before Kirri could speak. "I think what you're missing is the big picture."

"That's exactly what Ty said!" Kirri interjected.

"If more than one person you trust is telling you the exact same thing, do you think perhaps it's time to slow down and actually listen?"

She started to snap back a retort, then stopped herself.

Trust?

She trusted Lucius and she trusted Ty.

"So what did Ty say to you? Exactly. No embellishments, please."

She saluted at the phone. So many instructions. Then again, he was the first person—the *only* person—she'd thought of calling when her life had crumbled into a million tiny pieces.

"Okay, fine…" She huffed. "Here's *exactly* what he said."

When she'd finished, Lucius intoned, "For someone so smart you can really be clueless sometimes—you know that, Kirri?"

"Well, thank you very much." She sniffed.

"I didn't hear anything in there about you being hopeless, or incapable, or any of the self-flagellating insults you've no doubt heaped upon yourself."

"He said he wanted me to leave."

"He *said*," Lucius replied slowly, "that he wanted you to follow your dreams. He was being supportive."

"How on earth does he know what my dreams are?" she all but bellowed into the phone.

Lucius started laughing.

Kirri's hackles flew up another notch. "This is *not* funny."

Lucius, still laughing, asked, "You're in love with him, aren't you?"

Her heart flew into her throat. "How on earth did you—?"

"Oh, c'mon, Kirri. No one gets that upset when one of the most prestigious physicians in the pediatric world says one teeny-tiny thing they don't like. Does he love you?"

She choked out a no.

Lucius was silent for a minute, then asked, "Did he tell you as much?"

Again, she said no.

"Listen, K… It sounds to me as if he's trying to do everything right by you. Whereas I bulldoze in and tell you to stop your research, *he* says if that's what makes you happy go for it. If that isn't love…"

Kirri mulled it over. Lucius loved her in an

overprotective brotherly way. Even though it was annoying, it was strangely comforting. Whereas Ty...

She silently swore.

Ty knew more than anyone that life was for living. He was the last person on earth to stop someone from following their dreams, because he knew everyone only had one life to live.

Her stomach lurched. Could he have told her to pack her bags and leave because he *loved* her?

"Kirri? Are you still there?" Lucius didn't wait for her to answer. "What is it you really want? Is it research?"

No. No, it wasn't. It was to love Ty. Ty and Lulu. And the rest of his huge, wonderfully batty family.

More than that, she wanted to be able to give him a child. A sibling for Lulu. Several, if she could.

But she couldn't. No amount of medical breakthroughs would ever change that one brutal fact.

The thought hit her like a bulldozer.

That was what this was all about. A perverse Gift of the Magi. He was handing her the world he thought she wanted and the one thing she wanted to give him, she couldn't. Was it time to put herself out there? Dare to tell him how she really felt about him?

"I want to be with Ty," she said.

The trial run at admitting the truth felt good.

"I know," Lucius said gently.

"Who made *you* so wise?" She sniffled, and then said, "What on earth am I meant to do about it? He wants me to go to Vienna."

"As your big brother, it's my responsibility to help you see what you can't."

"Which is…?"

"Until you admitted as much you weren't ready to love him. Now it's time to believe in yourself. You're good enough. Just as you are. I know the baby thing kills you, but don't let it define you. You're worth loving. You don't need some hi-tech bells-and-whistles invention to prove you're a good person. You *are* a good person. One of the best."

Kirri felt as though her heart would burst. Her brother thought all those things about her? "But—but you told me you weren't going to let me continue."

"I know. I can be an ass, and I don't always have the best technique for communicating what I really want to say."

"What *do* you really want to say?"

"That I don't care that you were born the way you were. You're perfect just as you are. The research thing was a bandage for a wound you need to let heal. And you're going to have to find another way to make yourself feel whole."

The way she felt when she was with Ty.

Was giving up her research something she could do and still feel whole?

A fire lit in her belly so hot and fierce she instantly knew the answer. She needed to see Ty— to find out if she was the only who was measuring her personal worth in tandem with her value as a medical innovator.

It didn't matter two beans to her brother. And she knew there was no point in calling her father. He'd always be stuck in his ways, and some wounds… Some wounds were better left as scars that would remind a girl of just how far she'd come.

"So…" Kirri wiped away a few remaining tears. "Does this mean you've had my back all along?"

"Course I have. You're my little sister."

Her heart squeezed tight. Hearing him say that meant the world. "Lucius? Do you think leaving here would make me an idiot?"

"Pretty much."

She laughed. "I can still rely on you for total honesty, then, I see?"

"Always," he said, his voice infused with so much affection she felt as though she were receiving her first ever proper hug from him.

"Lucius?"

"Yes?"

"I love you."

"Love you too, kiddo. Now, go and tell your boyfriend you love him."

She didn't need telling twice.

CHAPTER ELEVEN

TY STOOD OUTSIDE Kirri's door and stared at the huge bouquet of flowers. It was the armload of Australian wildflowers Lulu had helped him select. Was this the right thing? For Kirri, for Lulu, for him?

Damn straight it was.

He moved his hand toward the door.

It opened before he made contact.

Kirri screamed.

Ty winced. "That wasn't quite the reaction I was hoping for."

Kirri pressed her hands to her chest as she composed herself. "Sorry. I wasn't expecting you to be there."

"I need to talk to you."

"Good." She looked him straight in the eye. "I need to talk to *you*."

Ty looked past her shoulder into the bedroom and saw the half-packed bag. His heart plummeted. Talking a headstrong woman into loving you for the rest of her life wasn't a skill he had in his arsenal.

"Packing's going well, I see."

Beautifully observed, Ty. Now, grow a pair! You've operated on twenty-week-old babies still inside their mothers. Tell her how you feel.

Kirri's dark lashes fluttered a moment, and her cheeks pinked up as her blue eyes met his again. She'd been crying. A lot, from the looks of things. She also looked a bit sheepish.

"Um…about that…"

And just like that a ray of hope lit his life up.

The flowers hit the ground. His heart pounded against his chest and in one long-legged stride he was cupping her face in his hands and tasting her sweet dusty-rose lips. Never before had a kiss felt so fortifying.

Her body language spoke volumes. The arm around his waist said *I love you.* Her hand on his heart said, *We are connected.* Her lips tasting and exploring his as if it were their very first kiss said *Never let me go.* He wouldn't. Not ever again. Whatever they needed to do to make this work…find time to explore the possibilities…he would do it.

After they'd held one another for a while she gave him a soft kiss and said, "I guess you've figured out I've struggled with making the right decision."

"It's a *very* big decision."

"Not if you know you're in love with a man in Atlanta."

Ty pulled Kirri close and held her tight. "I love you, too. I just want to do the best by you. Not stifle you with a life you don't want to lead."

Kirri pulled back and looked at him as if he was crazy. "I think we are both suffering from a severe case of getting hold of the wrong end of the stick."

"You were so excited about the research in Vienna. The professional advances you'd be able to make there, Kirri—they'd be huge."

She nodded, her eyes flicking away as she no doubt pictured the high-tech lab there.

"It's a huge decision. Especially when there's a child involved. A child who, by the way, picked out these." He scooped up the flowers and held them out to her with a small bow.

Kirri's eyes filmed over as she pressed her fingers to her mouth.

"Is…?" Ty's heart caught in his throat. "Is Lulu a problem?"

"No! I adore Lulu. She's amazing. But…"

"But…?" Ty's deepest fears turned the heat in his chest to ice in his veins.

"You know I'll never be able to give her a brother or sister—if things go that way."

"My love, I'm going into this with eyes wide open."

"What do you mean by that?"

Ty put the flowers on the breakfast bar, then turned to her. "No one is expecting you to make a final decision right here and now. About any of it. Vienna. Trying things with me. The changes you're facing are huge. Moving country. Continent, even. Loving me. My child."

"In fairness, the loving you and Lulu part is pretty easy," she confessed, with the first hint of a proper smile teasing at the corners of her mouth. "It's the lifestyle changes that go with it that have got me all twisted up inside."

Kirri traced a line down his arm, then pressed her hand to his cheek before she spoke again.

"I'm probably a bit too used to being impetuous. The plus side, I suppose, of having your big brother as your boss. He's relatively flexible about forgiveness."

The warmth in those blue eyes of hers told him something had shifted in her relationship with her brother. In the right direction.

"Not that you aren't flexible," she went on. "But you have Lulu to consider, and—and if you want a sibling for her that's impossible with me."

"Most things aren't entirely impossible," he said.

It was a weighted statement and they both

knew it. He was saying he was willing to explore adoption. Fostering. The possibility that Lulu would be an only child if that suited all three of them.

"But if you want to go to Vienna…you should go."

Her lip quivered. "I'm terrified that letting my research go will make you think less of me. It's how things work in my family. To get attention you have to *do* something. Something valuable. Lucius got the worst of it, being the son and heir and all that, but I always thought—" Her voice broke but she pushed on through. "I thought that if I couldn't give my parents grandchildren, maybe I could give them the kudos of having a daughter who'd achieved something no one else in the world had."

Ty's heart twisted tightly for her. How awful. To think that love came as part of a merit package.

"Kirri, I admire your work. It's incredible. But that's not how I think, darlin'. I love you for *you*. Hell…" He swept a lock of hair away from her cheek. "If you wanted to set up a peach pie stall I'd still love you. Or take bubble baths all day. Don't get me wrong—I'd love to have you on the surgical staff. That's what I can offer you, and I think you'd be a brilliant addition to the team.

But…and I may regret saying this… I'd still love you if you chose to stuff my offer in my face and move to Vienna, if you really thought that was what would make you happy. Long-distance relationships can work. Lulu's never been to Vienna. Nor have I."

Kirri looked at him in astonishment. "You'd consider a long-distance relationship?"

"I'd consider anything if it meant giving us more time to figure out what this is between us," Ty said, from the bottom of his heart. "Whatever you choose, know this: I have never once considered your inability to have children as a factor in whether or not I fall in love with you." He gave a self-effacing laugh. "If it makes you feel any better, I haven't been all that sure that anyone would be interested in falling in love with a widower surgeon whose life revolves around his nutty family."

Kirri started laughing. "Are you kidding me? That is one seriously smokin' hot package!"

Their laughter filled the room, replacing the pain they'd shared.

Ty took one of her hands in his and gave the back of it a kiss. "Look, it's up to you what you choose. I know how important your research is to you. But I'd hate to think that you believe what you do for a living defines who you are."

She threw him a quirky look. "Have you been on the phone with my brother?"

"No, but it sounds like we have a similar opinion." He slipped his fingers through her hair and tipped his forehead to hers to give her a soft kiss. "You are amazing. With or without all the wondrous things you do. Your heart, your soul, your generosity. Maybe not so much your bowling..."

She gave him a playful poke in the ribs.

"Kirri, *you* are who I'd love to have in our lives—not your certificates of achievement. But if Lulu isn't a priority for you..." He steadied his voice.

Damn, this was hard.

"Don't," Kirri cut in. "I know Lulu's happiness is paramount. I would never ask you to live life my way, especially if it would compromise her happiness. She's your number one girl." She spoke without envy. And with love in her voice she continued, "Lulu's your world."

"My world has room for you in it, too, Kirri. *And* my family's world. We all love you." He gave a self-effacing laugh. "I think I probably corner the market on loving you the most, but suffice it to say if there's anything I can do or say to convince you to consider being my girl—even if we have to push the boundaries in figuring out how it works—my heart is yours."

Kirri bit down on her lip, her eyes bright with

unshed tears. "It's just all so different to how I imagined finding my happiness."

"Not everything comes in the package we expect," he said.

"You can say that again!"

Kirri laughed and swept away a couple of tears that had lost their battle with gravity. She gave Ty a kiss, filled with gratitude that they were talking. She had spent so much of her life blinkering herself toward her mission to succeed—who knew how much *actual* life she'd missed? Moments like this. Honest, pure, loving moments when, if she was brave enough, she could change her life forever.

She ran her fingertips over Ty's dark stubble and traced her finger along his lips. When she reached the center he kissed them.

You'd be a fool to give this up for pride.

Many other men in his shoes—men with a daughter to protect and care for—would have shown her the door. Booked her airplane ticket themselves. But Ty was a cut above the rest, and he was willing to work with her to find a way for them to live happily together.

"All of this is finally making me realize that the things we *think* we want are not necessarily the best things for us." She leant back on the couch, hearing the astonishment in her own voice as she said, "I had a long talk with my big brooding brother and who knew? He's got a heart the size of Australia and it seems I was the last person to notice."

Ty ran his finger along the back of her hand for a moment, clearly gathering his thoughts. When he did speak, his voice hummed with an intensity she'd never heard from him before.

"As we're spilling our hearts here, you should know I've had my own learning curve to climb. When Gemma died, as you can imagine, my world fell to bits."

Kirri nodded. How could it not have?

"Before she passed I worked with an incredible surgeon as an intern. He knew everything about everything—or so I thought. He liked to do things by the book. *His* book. Safety first was his motto. If you followed the rulebook nothing could go wrong! Was I learning? Absolutely. But I was only learning how to do things *his* way."

Kirri chewed on the inside of her cheek, unsure where this was going.

"Anyway, I was working all the hours God sent. Then Gemma got her diagnosis, Lulu was born, Gemma lost her battle, and for a few months there I was utterly incapable of work. I didn't go in. *Couldn't* go in. The guilt I felt for having devoted myself to the hospital instead of treasuring the time we had together—" His voice caught in his throat but he pushed through. "I know I can't blame myself for not knowing Gemma's life would be so cruelly shortened, but I *can* blame myself for not having prioritized our lives over my work."

Kirri's heart ached to hear the pain in his voice, but something told her he was putting himself through this for a reason. For *her*.

"How did you get through it?" she asked.

He rubbed his thumb along the back of her hand and shot her a soft smile. "My family. A few tough-skinned friends. To be honest, I'd neglected the handful of friends I had left in those final few weeks Gemma and I had. And after she died I didn't want to see anyone. My mentor let me go. No blame there. He had to. Patients don't wait around for a widower to get his act together. In all honesty, if it hadn't been for my mother and sisters I'm sure Lulu wouldn't have heard a human voice for months."

"Oh, Ty. I'm so sorry you had to go through all of that."

He shook his head solidly. "Don't be. I won't say it doesn't hurt that Gemma died. It does, and it probably always will to an extent. But the thing I never expected was to be grateful for the darkness, because the light it has given me in return is something I wouldn't change for the world."

"I'm sorry. I don't understand…"

He brushed the backs of his fingers against her cheek. She so wanted to lean into him. Have him hold her tight. But he was telling her this story for a reason.

"Darlin', can't you see? If Gemma hadn't died, my life very likely would've stayed exactly as it was. I would've carried on with my shifts at the hospital, working for the same mentor. I was happy. We both were. We thought our lives were perfect just as they were. When she died—" he drew in a jagged breath "—I was forced to look at life from a different perspective."

Boy. That had to have been tough. Examining what had obviously been a perfect relationship and then figuring out how to come out of the wreckage after Gemma's death a better man.

Ty continued. "Years later than you I realized just how important it was to make a difference. Not just on a personal level, but on a professional level as well."

"How do you mean?"

"I mean I was living my professional life according to someone else's playbook. I did exactly what my mentor said, never questioning it."

The light began to dawn for Kirri. "We've basically approached life from opposite directions…"

Kirri's personal life had been pure wreckage, so she'd poured herself into forging new frontiers in her professional life, whilst Ty's personal life had been brilliant so he'd seen no need to change what he was doing professionally.

Life had pulled them together from opposite ends of the seesaw. Was now the time to prove they could find the perfect balance?

As if to prove her point, Ty continued. "Think of the lives that have been saved because I decided to look at surgery through my own eyes. Eyes that didn't want to see anyone else having to go through what I had. This is the example I'm trying to set for Lulu. This is why I offer the exchange program. To offer some fresh perspective. Sometimes all it takes is stepping out of your routine to realize whether or not it's working for you."

Kirri's chest filled with a tangle of emotions. She understood what he was saying. All work and no play was making Kirri an unhappy bunny. But was she prepared to drop all those years of hard work—years of wearing her research as a protective shield—to try something new?

"So…you think I *shouldn't* go to Vienna?"

"I'm trying to say this doesn't have to be a black and white scenario. We have options." He looked Kirri square in the eye. "The main question is, do we explore them or stick to what we know?"

Kirri began putting together what her brother had said with what Ty was trying to communicate.

Give this new life a chance.

"What was it that finally clicked for you? When you decided to start the Piedmont Women and Baby Pavilion?"

Ty answered solidly. "No matter what I did, or how I behaved, I wasn't going to get to live the life I thought I would be living with Gemma because there was nothing I could do to bring her back. My only choice was to stop craving what I couldn't have and get busy living the life I had."

The penny dropped—and as it did, the tears began to fall.

Ty pulled her into his arms. "Everything's going to be all right, darlin'. I promise."

"I know!" she sobbed. "It's just so hard."

"What is?"

"Letting go of the crutch I've been holding on to for so long."

"Your research?"

"Yup." She swept away another sheet of welcome tears. Welcome because for the first time they felt healing. "You're absolutely right. I've been avoiding my own life because I've been trying to live the one I'd never have."

She looked into Ty's eyes and saw encouragement and love. He was proof that joy could blossom out of sorrow. That there was life beyond a devastating blow. She had a cornucopia of blessings, and all she had to do was open up her arms and embrace them.

Eventually her breathing steadied. "I can't believe I've been so blind…"

Ty stroked her cheek with his thumb. "I wouldn't say blind. Let's call it 'not entirely focused'."

She giggled and wiped away yet more tears. A shift was happening inside her. One that would change her for the rest of her life if she was brave enough.

"So. What I need to do is live the life I have, knowing I'll never have a child of my own."

He nodded. "As cruel as it is, you won't get that life. You know that."

"I know…" she hiccupped. "I just thought… I thought if I worked hard enough…made a different kind of baby…"

"The baby grow bag?"

She nodded. "I thought if I made that and got my name on a door, or a plaque, or a trophy to put on a shelf, then the hole in me would be filled. But the truth is nothing will fill it. The same way, I suppose, that nothing will ever replace the love you had for Gemma."

"True. But there's no point in looking at the emptiness. What matters is what I *do* have." He went on with a big old smile on his face. "I have Lulu. I have the nuttiest family this side of the

Mississippi. And, if you'll have me, I sure as hell would love to have you in my life. Whichever way we can do it. I'd far rather try to make it work than give up now."

She nodded. "I would love that. But on one condition."

Ty's eyes narrowed. He was listening.

Kirri could hardly believe she was hearing the words that came out of her mouth. "Did you mean it about having me on the surgical staff?"

"What about your research?"

"I think I need to let that go."

"I would never ask that of you…"

"I know. But it's time."

A lightness she hadn't expected to feel filled her chest.

"To give it up completely?" Ty looked astonished. Happy. But amazed.

She tipped her head back and forth. "I think what I'd like to do is fly over to Vienna and share my findings with the team, then leave it with them."

There was an edge of doubt in his voice. "If that's what would truly make you happy…"

"You and Lulu make me happy."

Her answer elicited a broad, gorgeous smile. She steadied herself before asking the big question. The one that counted the most.

"Are you one hundred percent sure you'll never resent me for not being able to have a child?"

He shook his head. "Darlin', I never thought I'd fall in love again, let alone have another child. Having you in our lives is miracle enough. I love you exactly the way you are. If having more children had been an issue I never would've taken things as far as they've gone. We have Lulu. We're perfect as we are. A family."

We. A family.

Her heart skipped a beat. "Is adoption something you'd ever consider?" she asked.

Ty brushed his thumb along her cheek. "In all honesty, I hadn't thought of it because I didn't have you. It's not something I'd rule out, though. Or fostering." He dropped a kiss on her forehead. "Listen, there's a whole world of possibilities that can open up for us, but I think we need to do this as clear-eyed as possible. You need to go to Vienna and see what's there, and then we'll get on with living our lives the best we can."

He was right. It was time. Time to trust. Time to love.

CHAPTER TWELVE

"RIGHT, THEN." Ty hung up his phone and gave Lulu his best reassuring smile. "He hasn't heard from her since she left for the airport."

Lulu's eyebrows dove together. "But she's coming back, right?"

She was. She'd sent him the itinerary. But he was feeling a bit like his daughter right now. Seeing was believing.

"Lucius said she was." He ruffled his daughter's hair, much to her annoyance. Fair enough. They were both edgy. "Lucius said she was very clear about the fact he should hire a replacement, so…"

"So that means she's coming to Atlanta to stay!" Lulu beamed. "And did you ask the question?"

"I did."

"Did he say yes?"

"He said…" Ty cleared his throat and put on an appalling version of an Australian accent. "It wasn't his place to say yes, and his sister would do as she jolly well pleased."

Lulu clapped her hands. "I'm going to have an uncle who lives Down Under!"

Ty laughed and pulled her into his arms for a quick cuddle, so she wouldn't see the nerves that were tugging his forehead closer to the bridge of his nose.

He and Kirri had agreed not to speak whilst she was in Vienna. It seemed insane now, given the fact he'd told her he wanted nothing more than for her to be in their lives each and every day. But showing her he would support her even if she did suddenly decide she needed to work in Austria had seemed paramount.

He'd been shocked when she'd rung him after a week to say she needed to go to Sydney. They'd tried to talk again, but with the time difference and his work, and childcare demands, their conversations had never got beyond some quick *I'm fine... I love you* chats.

"Not yet, you don't. Right, then, little one. Shall we go get some barbecue?"

Lulu heaved a dramatic sigh. "It's more fun when Kirri's there."

"Only one more sleep until she's back, sweetheart."

And he hoped to God all the sleeps from there on out would be together.

"Okay, Daddy. Let's get this show on the road!"

Lulu marched out of the house and down to the car as if she were in a parade.

He smiled at the doorframe as he locked up. The last time he'd carried Kirri through this door he'd had no idea whether their futures would intertwine or not. The next time he carried her through it he hoped more than anything she'd be wearing a white dress.

Kirri looked at her phone. She was fifteen minutes early, but that didn't mean Ty wouldn't arrive any minute now. It was Tuesday night and that meant only one thing: barbecue, biscuits and bowling.

"Checking your watch every five seconds isn't going to make him come any faster, honey."

Kirri grinned sheepishly at Chuck, and then at the house specialty, a plate of fried green beans with a bit of ranch dip on the side he was slipping onto the checkered-cloth-covered table.

"You trying to give me a heart attack while I wait?" she asked.

Chuck laughed and gave her shoulder a squeeze. "Nah, honey. I'm giving you some extra special soul food to keep that smile on your face. Good to have you back."

"It's good to be here."

She meant it, too. Her week in Vienna had been

absolutely amazing. The team there had been astonished at how far she'd come doing research on her own and with limited resources. They'd said if she wanted to stay they'd find a way to make it happen. What had amazed her had been her response.

"No, thank you. I'm busy with a new project now."

A project that involved relocating to Atlanta to see if she could build a new life with a man who'd made her see that she was worth loving just as she was.

She glanced at the doorway, willing him to appear.

"You been away to Australia?" asked Chuck.

She nodded. "And Vienna."

"Vienna!" Chuck looked impressed. "What on earth were you doing there?"

"Finding out that I wanted to live here."

Chuck laughed. "Honey, I coulda told you that the first day you walked in here."

Kirri's eyes widened.

"Oh, don't give me those big ol' blue eyes of yours. He was looking at you the same way you were looking at him. And don't try to deny it. I've been round the block enough to know lovey-dovey looks when they're right in front of me."

Kirri held up her hands with a grin. "Guilty."

He was right. The moment she'd handed her

research over to the elite team of scientists in Vienna her heart had told her exactly what she wanted to do. Get on a plane and come back home.

She'd swung by Sydney, to wrap things up there, to sell her apartment. Help Lucius hire a replacement. Give him the big old hug she'd been dying to give him ever since they'd had their heart-to-heart.

And then she'd packed up a few bags and got on a plane.

She crossed her fingers and stared at the door. Just a few more minutes and she'd know if she'd made the right call.

Lulu ran out of the car and into the restaurant the second Ty parked outside of Chuck's. Before he had locked the car door he could hear her sweet little voice whooping, "She's here, she's here, she's *here*!"

Ty's heart bashed against his chest as his keys jammed against the little black box in his pocket. He'd picked it up earlier and had been going to triple-check with Lulu that she was happy for Kirri to come into their lives permanently—but it looked like things were moving ahead of schedule.

He shifted his keys to the other pocket. He didn't want a single thing to get in the way. There had been enough hurdles. Enough wondering. Enough emptiness in his life to know he'd finally found a woman worth taking a risk for.

Kirri and Lulu appeared in the doorway.

"Daddy...?" Lulu was looking at him curiously.

Kirri's eyes were sparkling with the exact same glint of recognition they'd had when they'd very first met. Soulmates.

"How was your trip?" he asked.

Kirri grinned at him. "It was great."

"The I'm-returning-to-Vienna kind of great?"

She slowly shook her head, that smile of hers spreading from ear to ear. "The I'm-returning-to-Atlanta kind of great."

Words failed him. He pulled her into his arms and hugged her close, her sweet citrusy scent filling the air around them.

He dropped a soft kiss onto her lips. "I love you. I missed you so much it actually hurt. Lulu and I—" He pulled his daughter over by his side and gave her a squeeze. "We didn't really know what to do with ourselves when you were away, so we went shopping. Ring shopping."

Kirri's eyes glossed over with tears as Lulu jumped up and down with excitement. "You did?"

Ty nodded. "We did."

"Do you want to know what I did?" Kirri asked.

The look in her eyes and the warmth in her voice told him he definitely did want to know.

"Lay it on us," he said.

"I packed."

He twirled his finger around. "More information please, darlin'. You're killing me here."

She laughed and gave Lulu's head an affectionate scrub. "I handed over my research and I packed up my apartment in Sydney… To move here. If the offer still stands?"

Ty pulled out the small black box and flicked the lid open so she could see the ring they'd chosen. "Would this answer your question?"

Kirri's hands flew to her mouth. "Oh, Ty! It's amazing."

They all looked at the ring. White gold, with a halo of diamonds around an Australian black opal.

"It's absolutely beautiful."

Ty smiled as Lulu explained. "We went to *all* of the jewelers and said it had to remind you of home."

"Oh, it definitely does."

Kirri held out her hand as Ty slipped the ring onto her finger. It fit perfectly. And when she looked into Ty's eyes she saw nothing but love in them.

"So…can I take that as a yes?" he asked.

"You most definitely can."

Lulu squealed with delight and ran into the restaurant, where they could hear her announcing the happy news that her daddy was going to have a wife.

"You're a hundred percent sure?" Ty asked.

"I've never been more sure of anything," Kirri said, tilting her face up to seal their engagement with another perfect kiss.

* * * * *

BᴠB

*Look out for the next story in the
Miracles in the Making duet*

The Neonatal Doc's Baby Surprise
by Susan Carlisle

*And if you enjoyed this story, check out
these other great reads from
Annie O'Neil*

Making Christmas Special Again
A Return, a Reunion, a Wedding
The Doctor's Marriage for a Month
Tempted by Her Single Dad Boss

All available now!